6/92

Hot Competition

At lunch Samantha tried to explain to Brittany why she had gone after the TV host spot, too. "Look, Brittany, I really need an activity for my school record. Besides, you know how awful I've felt since Kyle broke up with me. This show will help me take my mind off him."

Brittany was too angry to care. "What gave you the idea that you were a journalist? The only newspapers you ever read are the trashy tabloids at the supermarket!"

"Come on, you guys," Kim interrupted. "Why don't you just take it easy? I mean, this is a little friendly competition, not a war."

Brittany ignored her and kept her eyes fixed on Samantha. "You don't stand a chance, you know. I'm going to get that job. You might as well give up now before you're totally humiliated."

"I came here and apologized so we could be friends again," Samantha said. She shoved back her chair and stood up. "I take back my apology. I'm going to win that part. You want a fight, Brittany? You've got one!"

Books in the RIVER HEIGHTS ® Series

Available from ARCHWAY Paperbacks

River HEIGHTS™ #15

FRIENDS AND RIVALS

CAROLYN KEENE

AN ARCHWAY PAPERBACK
Published by POCKET BOOKS
New York   London   Toronto   Sydney   Tokyo   Singapore

AN ARCHWAY PAPERBACK *Original*

An Archway Paperback published by
POCKET BOOKS, a division of Simon & Schuster Inc.
1230 Avenue of the Americas, New York, NY 10020

ISBN: 0-671-73119-X

First Archway Paperback printing March 1992

10 9 8 7 6 5 4 3 2 1

1

"Sugar, we need to have a little chat." Samantha Daley's father folded the morning paper and tucked it under the rim of his plate. "I know you've got school and I have to get to the office, but I promise this won't take long."

Samantha kissed her father on the cheek and sat down at the breakfast table. "Sure, Daddy, what is it?"

Samantha's mother poured Samantha some orange juice and brought it to the table. "Honey, your father and I are starting to get just a teeny bit worried," she said. Mrs. Daley was an older version of her daughter, with cinnamon-colored hair and brown eyes. She was wearing a flowing turquoise caftan and about a dozen silver bracelets that jan-

gled wildly whenever she moved her hands.
All the Daleys had southern accents, having
moved to River Heights from the South, but
Mrs. Daley's was the strongest. "You know
how we love you," she said, "and sometimes
—well, we just can't help worrying."

Uh-oh, Samantha thought. This sounded
serious. She sipped her juice and tried to
remember if she'd done anything wrong lately. Broken her curfew? No. Spent too much
money on clothes? Probably, but her mother
wouldn't be worried about that. Lavonne
Daley loved clothes almost as much as
Samantha did. Her father might grumble
about the bills, but he wouldn't take time out
to have a "little chat" about it. Nothing else
came to mind. "What is it?" Samantha asked
again, reaching for a piece of toast.

"I'll come right to the point," her father
said. "College."

Oh. Samantha got it now. Her father had
talked to her a while back about bringing her
grades up and participating in extracurricular activities that would look good on her
high school transcript. She hadn't exactly
forgotten, but college was hardly the most
important thing on her mind.

"You know, honey," Mrs. Daley said,
"you *are* a junior. It's time to start thinking
about the future."

"Your mother's right." Samantha's father

took a sip of coffee. "You can go to just about any college you want, money-wise. But first you have to get accepted."

"I know, Daddy." Samantha was definitely not in the mood for this. Everything was crashing down on her. Her boyfriend, Kyle Kirkwood, had broken up with her only the week before. That was bad enough, but what made it even worse was that it was all her fault.

Kyle had written a computer program to match couples for the junior class's Hawaiian luau. Samantha had fiddled with it and matched Kyle with the one person she'd thought would be perfectly safe and harmless—Sasha Lopez. Wrong! Kyle and Sasha were now a sizzling twosome, and Samantha was out in the cold. After all she'd done for Kyle, too—suggesting the right clothes and haircut, changing him from a nerd into someone very cool. And now Sasha had him. It was totally humiliating. After Samantha lost Kyle, she realized how much she really had cared about him. How could she possibly think about college at a time like this?

Samantha took a bite of toast, racking her brain for anything in her favor to prove to her father she was trying. "Well," she said finally, "I did get a B on my last research paper in social studies. And I pulled a B minus on a chemistry quiz." She didn't mention that she'd still probably wind up with C's in both subjects.

"Wonderful!" Samantha's mother beamed. "Isn't that exciting, John?"

"I knew you could do it, sugar," Mr. Daley said approvingly. "Now, what about some extracurricular activities? They can't hurt, you know, especially if your grades aren't top-notch. Colleges really go for that kind of thing."

Samantha nodded. She knew she ought to do *something*—not just for college, but because she was so restless. She was definitely ready for something new, but the only things that came to mind were new clothes and a new boyfriend. It would be impossible to get Kyle back, she knew that. Even if Sasha weren't in the picture now, Kyle had made it clear that he was finished with Samantha. She wasn't quite over Kyle yet, but it would be nice to start dating again. It would help her forget Kyle and show him that he wasn't the only guy at River Heights High.

Unfortunately, shopping and dating weren't the kinds of extracurricular things you could put on your high school record. "Don't worry," Samantha said to her parents. "I'll find something to join, I promise." She crossed her heart and beamed at them.

That seemed to satisfy them—at least for the moment. Mr. Daley finished his coffee and headed off for work. Mrs. Daley rushed upstairs to change for her Monday morning aerobics class.

Gathering her books together, Samantha went out to catch the bus. She had been riding with her friend Kim Bishop, but Kim had just gotten back together with Jeremy Pratt, and they wanted to be alone all the time now. As the smelly bus lumbered toward school, Samantha tried to think of some club she could join.

Sports were out. She wasn't athletic enough to be on any team. Computers? Ha! Samantha didn't want to go near one for the rest of her life. Art? No, that was Sasha Lopez's territory.

Some committee, maybe, a one-shot deal. Then she wouldn't actually have to join a club and go to boring meetings for the rest of the year.

By the time the bus arrived at school, Samantha had decided to go the committee route. Brittany Tate, one of her best friends, wrote for the school paper, the *Record*. Brittany would have the inside track on any new committee that was forming. Of course, Brittany might not be thrilled about helping Samantha out. Brittany and Kim were still a little mad at Samantha. Even though it wasn't true, Brittany and Kim were sure that Samantha had switched their dates for the luau, using Kyle's computer, too.

Samantha got off the bus and walked toward the quad, searching for Brittany. As usual, the quad was filled with groups of kids waiting for the bell. Emily Van Patten and Bill Hutchins were standing under a tree. They'd been paired off at the luau, and now were dating pretty steadily. Emily looked happy. She also looked as if she'd lost some of the weight she'd put on. She was starting to look like her gorgeous model self again. At least the luau had been good for somebody, Samantha thought.

Farther on, Samantha passed Nikki Masters and her boyfriend, Tim Cooper. They were talking with Lacey Dupree and her boyfriend, senior Tom Stratton. Lacey had gone with Tom's brother, Rick, but then Rick had hooked up with someone named Katie, who went to Southside High. Tom and Rick had had a major fight about Lacey's dating Tom. That's what Samantha had heard, anyway. Not that she cared. But she couldn't help feeling a little jealous. Everywhere she looked there were couples.

Well, not everywhere. Pudgy Phyllis Bouchard was standing a few feet away from Nikki and her friends, gazing adoringly at Tim Cooper. Phyllis had been matched with Tim for the luau. She'd been walking around with her head in the clouds ever since.

Samantha kept walking. There was Teresa D'Amato, talking with Ben Newhouse and his girlfriend, Karen Jacobs. Terry seemed a little uncomfortable, as if she knew she was a third wheel.

Samantha slowed down as Teresa's situation hit her. Was that how *she* looked now without Kyle? Like somebody who didn't fit in?

No, that was ridiculous. Samantha knew she could find another guy. Not someone to fall in love with maybe—she wasn't ready for that yet. But there were plenty of guys she could date. In fact, a committee was the perfect place to find a boyfriend.

Cheered by that idea, Samantha started walking briskly again. Up ahead were Kim Bishop and supersnob Jeremy Pratt with their arms wrapped around each other. Every time Samantha saw them lately, they'd been in a clinch.

"Well, well," Samantha said loudly as she moved up behind them. "If it isn't River Heights High's happiest couple."

Startled, Kim pulled away from Jeremy. Then she blushed and smoothed her blond hair into place. "Hi, Samantha," she said.

"Have you seen Brittany?" Samantha said. "I thought she'd be out here."

"She's inside," Kim said. "Somebody died."

Samantha gasped. "Who?"

"Jackson Caldwell," Jeremy said, his blond head an almost perfect match for Kim's.

Samantha stared at him blankly.

"The third," Jeremy added as if that explained everything.

"The third what?" Samantha asked. Jeremy was such a jerk. She could hardly stand him, but he obviously made Kim happy. "Did this Jackson guy go here? I've never heard of him."

"He used to go here, about sixty years ago," Kim told her.

"You've never heard of the Caldwells?" Jeremy looked down his narrow nose at Samantha. "They've been in River Heights for generations."

"Well, I've only been here a few years," Samantha reminded him. "Anyway, what does Jackson Caldwell have to do with Brittany?"

"She and DeeDee are writing an article about him for the *Record*," Kim said. DeeDee Smith was a senior and the newspaper's editor-in-chief. "I don't know all the details, but Mr. Caldwell donated to the school some kind of closed-circuit television setup in his will. Tutoring on tape, stuff like that."

"It's much, much bigger than that!" Brittany Tate said excitedly as she strolled up behind them. She tossed her glossy dark hair off her shoulders and her breath came out in tiny white clouds as she spoke. "You know Mr. Weston, the audiovisual teacher?"

Everyone nodded.

"Well, he's in charge of this whole thing," Brittany said, "and he was just talking to DeeDee and me about it. Guess what? River Heights High is going to have its own television show!"

"What's it going to be?" Kim asked dryly. "'Trig in Five Easy Lessons'? 'Tips on studying for the SATs'?"

Brittany shook her head. "No, you don't get it. This is going to be a magazine-type news show, like 'River Heights This Week,'" she said, referring to a popular local television program. "It hasn't all been worked out yet, but we'll be doing things like interviewing students and teachers, maybe taping parts of classes, stuff like that. Mr. Weston is the advisor, but the show's going to be totally run by students."

Jeremy brushed an invisible piece of lint off the sleeve of his down jacket. "Every video freak in school's going to be crawling out of the woodwork."

Brittany ignored him. "And here's the best part," she said. "The show's going to have two hosts—a guy and a girl."

Kim grinned. "Now I know why you're so excited," she said. "You're going to be the girl host, right?"

"Well, I do have to try out first," Brittany said with a modest laugh. "We're going to have a big meeting tomorrow after school for everybody who's interested in working on the show. I'm sure I won't be the only girl going after the host spot." She narrowed her dark eyes and smiled confidently. "But I am a journalist, after all. And DeeDee's one of the executive producers, so she'll be voting on the hosts. That's two points in my favor."

"Hmm," Samantha said thoughtfully. "The meeting's tomorrow?"

Brittany nodded.

"This is perfect. My parents are on my case about extracurricular activities," Samantha said. "If I tell them I'm working on a TV show they'll be thrilled."

"You don't know anything about television," Kim said bluntly.

Samantha didn't answer. She'd just spotted Kyle and Sasha, walking across the quad. They were holding hands and laughing. Kyle looked great, in faded jeans and a dark purple jacket. He would never have worn anything like that if it hadn't been for her, Samantha thought with a pang.

Sasha was pretty, but she didn't wear makeup and almost always dressed in black. Samantha guessed she was trying to be artsy looking, but as far as she was concerned, Sasha always looked like she was on her way to a funeral.

"You're right, I don't know anything about television," Samantha said, turning back to Kim. "But every TV show has somebody doing wardrobe and makeup, right?"

Samantha looked down at her black suede boots, which she was wearing with tight black leggings and an oversize hooded sweater in burnt orange. Over it all she had flung a buffalo plaid cape in orange and black. If there was one thing she did know, Samantha told herself, it was how to look good. Besides, she had a feeling the TV show was going to attract more than just video freaks. She'd bet money that lots of guys were going to be working on this project. Jackson Caldwell III would never know it, but he'd just given Samantha Daley a way to get her parents off her back and a whole new territory for boyfriend hunting.

By lunchtime everyone had heard about Mr. Caldwell's donation, and the cafeteria was buzzing with talk of the student-run television show. As she carried her tray to a table, Terry D'Amato heard kids talking about who the two hosts would be and which teachers they'd like to see interviewed. Terry wasn't interested in working on the show herself, but the whole project sounded kind of exciting.

When she finally reached her friends Ellen Ming and Karen Jacobs, Terry plunked her tray on their table and pulled out a chair to sit down. "I think River Heights has video fever," she said.

"It's great, isn't it?" Karen said. "You

know what Ben thinks?'' Ben Newhouse was junior class president and Karen's boyfriend. ''He thinks I should try out for the girl host spot. He said I'd be great on camera.'' She tucked her brown hair behind her ears and smiled happily. ''I know I'm more of a behind-the-scenes kind of person, but Ben thinks I can do anything.''

''That's love talking. Isn't it fantastic?'' Ellen's dark silky hair swung gently forward as she laughed. ''Kevin does that, too,'' she said, referring to her boyfriend, Kevin Hoffman, the student council vice president. ''He makes me feel so special. You know that horrible rain we had Saturday night? Well, Kevin and I got caught in it. By the time we got to his car, my hair was plastered to my head and my mascara was running down my cheeks. But Kevin said I looked beautiful.''

''Where did you two go?'' Karen asked. ''Ben and I thought we'd run into you at the movies, but we didn't see you.''

''The line was miles long, and we were both starving,'' Ellen said. ''So we went for pizza at Leon's. Then we rented a tape and watched it at my house.''

While Ellen and Karen went on about their weekend, Terry unwrapped her tuna sandwich and started eating. She knew her friends weren't *trying* to make her feel left out and jealous, but that was exactly how she felt. Every day, but especially on Mondays, when Ben and Kevin had a different lunch period, she had to listen to Karen and Ellen tell about the great times they'd had with their boyfriends over the weekend.

It wouldn't be so bad, Terry thought, if she were in between boyfriends or something. She'd still feel left out, but at least she'd know what they were talking about. The problem was, Terry had never had a boyfriend. For a long time, she hadn't cared, but now she *was* interested. Her braces were off, and she'd lost almost fifteen pounds. She wasn't bad looking, with dark brown hair and big eyes to match. She was pretty smart, too. No guys were exactly beating a path to her doorstep, though. Terry didn't know what it was like to hold hands with a guy or exchange private smiles with him. She'd never even been kissed!

Lots of times she'd thought of asking Karen and Ellen for advice, but it was just so humiliating, she couldn't bring herself to do it. She'd read every article she could about how to attract a boy, but when it came to actually trying, her mind would go blank.

"I can't believe it," Ellen said, breaking into Terry's thoughts. "It's already time to get to class. Did the clocks speed up or something?"

Time flies when you're in love, Terry thought, finishing the last of her lunch.

"We've been babbling on this whole time,"

Karen said apologetically to Terry. "I meant to call you on Sunday, but Ben and I decided to take a drive out to the lake. How was your weekend?"

"Oh, you know," Terry said. "The usual." She didn't mention that the usual was studying, watching a rented movie, grocery shopping, cleaning her room, and helping with the laundry. "It went by too fast, though. I can't wait for next weekend."

Maybe by then she'd have a boyfriend, Terry thought to herself. Ha! In her dreams!

 **2**

Brittany took a long, slow look around the audiovisual room. It was Tuesday after school, and the AV room was packed with at least fifty kids interested in working on the television show. For once, Brittany ignored the guys. She was too busy sizing up the girls. At least half of them, probably more, would be her competition for the host job.

Deanna Jordan, a senior with a flawless complexion and eyes the color of cut emeralds, was sitting two rows ahead, talking to a friend about trying out for the host. Brittany leaned forward to check out Deanna's profile, looking for imperfections. Even her nose was beautiful! Couldn't the girl at least have a pimple?

As if she felt herself being watched, Deanna turned around and caught Brittany's eye. "Hi," she said in a high-pitched, little-girl voice. "This is so exciting, isn't it?"

"It sure is," Brittany agreed happily. She sat back with a satisfied smile on her face. Looks weren't everything, thank goodness. And even if Deanna got straight A's, that Kewpie-doll voice made her sound about as bright as mud. She'd be out of the running the minute she opened her mouth.

"Hey, Brittany!" Cassie Morgenstern cried, stepping over Brittany's feet in pursuit of an empty chair. Brittany had piled her books on the chairs on either side of her, saving them for Kim and Samantha. "Are you here to try out for the host job, too?"

"I thought I'd take a shot at it." Brittany gave what she hoped was a carefree laugh. "I see I'm not the only one, though."

"Nope. I guess a lot of us suddenly wanted to find out if we're star material." Cassie spotted an empty chair and headed for it. "Good luck, Brittany!"

"Mmm," Brittany mumbled, watching the sophomore's departing back. Cassie was very slender, which was supposed to be good on camera. Her hair was great, too—a bunch of short, glossy brown curls that bounced when she walked. In fact, Cassie was a bouncy person, always happy and smiling and jumping up and down whenever she was excited. Too cheerleaderish, Brittany decided.

Scanning the competition again, Brittany spotted Karen Jacobs. Ha, Brittany thought. If Karen was going to go for the host spot, she'd better be prepared to lose graciously. Brittany had to admit that Karen had more confidence now that she was dating Ben Newhouse. Her looks had definitely improved, but it was all a matter of degree. Up against Brittany, Karen was as bland as vanilla pudding. Besides, Karen worked on the *Record.* How could she possibly expect to handle two big jobs at once? The fact that Brittany would have two big jobs if she became the host was beside the point. Brittany was used to juggling five or six situations at once.

Brittany noted a few more girls she might have to worry about, including Emily Van Patten. Emily was definitely looking great. She was someone to worry about.

"Hi, has anything happened yet?" Samantha asked as she and Kim joined Brittany. "I had to wait for Kim and Jeremy to say goodbye." She rolled her eyes. "Passion in the hallway!"

Kim's pale complexion suddenly got rosy. "He just kissed me," she said.

"For Preppy Pratt to do anything but shake hands in public is passionate," Samantha retorted.

"You're just jealous," Kim said. Then she

bit her lip. "Sorry," she said. "I didn't mean that. I know you're still feeling rotten about Kyle."

"Rotten is the word, all right," Samantha said with a sigh.

"You've got to stop thinking about him," Brittany advised. "There are plenty of other guys around."

"That's exactly why I'm here," Samantha said, glancing around the crowded room. "I figured there had to be plenty of gorgeous guys interested in working on a TV show." She turned back to Kim. "Why are you here, anyway? I didn't think you'd be interested in this."

"I'm not," Kim said with a shrug. "I'm just curious. Besides, Jeremy had to meet his father at the club, and I didn't feel like going home yet."

Samantha looked at Brittany. "So what's going on? Have you checked out the competition?"

"No. I've just been sitting here, waiting for things to get started," Brittany replied.

"Oh, sure." Kim gave Brittany a knowing look with her cool blue eyes. "Well, anyway, Nikki Masters isn't here. You must be relieved about that."

Brittany frowned. She hated to be reminded of Nikki-Always-Perfect-Masters. Nikki had everything—looks, money, brains, and Tim Cooper for a boyfriend. Plus, the girl was nauseatingly nice. She was probably too busy learning her lines for the next school play to try out. Brittany pushed Nikki straight out of her mind.

When the room was jammed with far too many people, Mr. Weston, the audiovisual teacher, came in. With him were DeeDee Smith and Robbie Bodeen, another senior.

Samantha poked Brittany in the arm. "How come Robbie and DeeDee get to be the producers?" she asked.

"Because Robbie's president of the media club and DeeDee's got a lot of organizational experience," Brittany said. "The project needs to get going fast."

Mr. Weston cleared his throat. He was a tall man with dark hair and eyes and a booming voice. "This is quite a turnout," he said, obviously pleased. "I know everybody's excited about the show, and I think it'll be an excellent way for all of you to get some hands-on experience."

The teacher smiled. "Mr. Caldwell's donation will allow us to put monitors all over the school. We'd like to have a monitor in each homeroom so daily announcements could be made over them. Aside from the news show, there are plans in the works for doing tutoring on tape and producing an electronic yearbook next year."

Mr. Weston cleared his throat again. "Now, before I turn the meeting over to

DeeDee and Robbie, just let me say that this news show is going to be run entirely by you, the students. I'll be here to offer advice and help, but the work—and the rewards—will be yours." He turned to DeeDee. "Why don't you carry on from here?" he said.

DeeDee, tall and slim in jeans and a mustard-colored sweater, moved to the front of the room. "Hi," she said, in a quiet voice that still managed to carry to the farthest seat. "I'm DeeDee Smith, and I'm going to be the executive producer. I'll help Robbie with some preproduction stuff, like choosing the hosts, but since I'm busy running the *Record,* Robbie's going to be the one you'll deal with most of the time." She glanced at Robbie Bodeen, a wiry senior with sandy blond spiked hair. Robbie was bouncing slightly on the balls of his feet, as if he had too much energy to remain still.

"Lots of you, I know, have already signed up to write for the show," DeeDee said. "It's going to be a magazine-type format, but we don't want fluff. No cute segments on miniskirts or peeks into the locker rooms. No staged food fights. We want solid, serious, hard-hitting news." She took in the whole room with one sweeping glance. "First, though, we need a name for the show," she said. "Why don't you throw out some ideas and we can vote today and get that settled?"

"'RHH Today,'" someone called.

"Nice," DeeDee said. "I like it. And I thought of 'Chalk Talk.' Any more?"

A girl suggested "Free Forum," and someone else came up with "River Heights High Almanac."

Robbie, who'd been bouncing faster and faster, finally shot forward and blurted out, "Hey, wait a sec. Hard-hitting? No problem, Dee. But no talking heads, either. Talking heads—everybody goes to sleep." Robbie spoke in little explosive jabs as if he couldn't get the words out fast enough. "TV's a visual medium, right?" he said. "We gotta have some fun with our show, give it some glitz, keep it snappy." He pointed at DeeDee, forming a pistol with his thumb and forefinger. "How's this for a name?" He bent his finger as if pulling the trigger. "'Fast Takes'?"

"Glitz?" DeeDee stared at him as if he were a mutated specimen in the science lab. "This isn't music television, Robbie. This is a news show with a magazine format. 'Fast Takes' makes it sound sleazy and cheap."

"Trust me, Dee," Robbie said. "I know video. I've been into it since junior high. It doesn't matter what the show is, you gotta grab the audience right up front, and you gotta use everything—sound, music, quick cuts. If we don't do that, the show'll go belly-up."

DeeDee took a deep breath. "Well, I've

been in journalism since junior high, Robbie, and I don't think a serious, solid journalistic show will go belly-up.''

Robbie shrugged. "Without the glitz, it'll be dead in the water, guaranteed."

"Ooh," Kim whispered to Brittany. "It's the battle of the producers. And I thought this would be boring."

Mr. Weston finally stepped in, smiling. "I knew when I chose both of you that there would be conflicts," he said to DeeDee and Robbie. "But consider this a learning process. You both want to go into broadcasting, and you're going to have to work with people who have different opinions. Part of becoming a professional is to learn how to resolve conflicts without hurting the show."

DeeDee smiled tightly at Robbie. "It isn't just our show, anyway," she said. "Let's vote on a name."

"A vote's fine with me," Robbie said.

The crowd voted by a show of hands. Robbie's title, "Fast Takes," was called first. Brittany liked it better than "Chalk Talk" or any of the others. But with DeeDee staring at her, she couldn't raise her hand. She'd need DeeDee's vote for the host job, and she couldn't afford to cross her now. When "Chalk Talk" was called, Brittany was one of five people to vote for it.

DeeDee took her defeat graciously, but it was obvious she wasn't happy with the way things were going. Next, she talked about how many stories they should do on the show. She wanted one in-depth segment and one shorter one. Robbie wanted at least four segments in every twenty-minute show.

"That's only five minutes a segment," DeeDee said in exasperation. "You can't get out any information in five minutes."

"Ever watch a commercial?" Robbie asked. "They get plenty of info in sixty seconds, even thirty. In video, five minutes is a lifetime." He ran his fingers through his spiky hair.

DeeDee raised her eyes to the ceiling. "I think she's counting to ten," Kim whispered.

"I don't blame her," Samantha whispered back. "Robbie's a pain."

Finally DeeDee spoke again. "I think we can work this out with the writing staff, Robbie. After all, this is just the beginning. We don't even have hosts or a crew yet. Why don't we post sign-up sheets and let everybody get their names on them. We'll let you know about another meeting soon."

"A-okay," Robbie said.

Still obviously annoyed with Robbie, DeeDee tacked the sheets on the bulletin board. She turned around and addressed the group once more. "Auditions will be tomorrow during the day. Please sign up to come for your free period."

"I was supposed to be at work five minutes ago, so I've got to hurry," Brittany said to Kim and Samantha, as kids began surging toward the bulletin board. Brittany sometimes worked after school at her mother's flower shop. "Catch you tomorrow."

"I'll go with you," Kim said. "I saw a pair of suede boots at the mall I want to try on."

Samantha said goodbye to her friends and stayed in her chair for a few minutes, waiting for the crowd to thin out. She wasn't in any hurry. Besides, it was a good opportunity to check out the guys.

Samantha watched as Brittany gracefully jostled through a group of kids to sign up for the host tryouts. Lots of the guys looked as if they still belonged in middle school. Samantha also rejected the obvious video freaks, guys who stood around talking about cross-fades and booms and dolly shots. A date with a techie would put her to sleep in five minutes.

Suddenly Samantha sat up a little straighter. There was Dylan Tager. She didn't know him, but she'd seen him plenty of times. Dylan, a senior, was impossible to ignore. Brown hair, golden brown eyes, a perfect build. And as far as Samantha knew, no girlfriend at the moment.

Gathering her books up, Samantha made her way to the bulletin board, where she managed to squeeze in next to Dylan. He was signing up to try out for the male host. Of course, she thought. Those looks would be wasted behind the camera.

When Dylan turned around, Samantha had a smile ready. "Hi," she said. "I'm looking for the sign-up sheet for makeup and wardrobe. Did you happen to see it?"

Dylan stared at her intently for a few seconds, his brown eyes searching her face. Finally he asked, "Do I know you?"

"No, but I know *you,*" Samantha said with a soft little laugh.

Dylan peered at her again. Then he smiled, and Samantha thought she might melt. "Sorry," he said. "I just can't—"

"Oh, I didn't mean we knew each other," Samantha said quickly. "I just meant I know who you are. I'm Samantha Daley."

"Samantha," Dylan said slowly.

Samantha waited. Was he trying to memorize her name or something? "Right, Samantha Daley," she said again. "I'm a junior," she added.

"Oh." Dylan smiled again. "Well, good luck, Samantha."

"On what?"

"Aren't you trying out for one of the host spots?"

Samantha blinked. Hadn't she just asked him about makeup and wardrobe? Before she could decide whether he'd forgotten or he was just a gorgeous dimwit, she felt a hand on her shoulder.

"Sure she is," Robbie Bodeen said, squeezing her shoulder. "I spotted you out there, Sammy," he went on. "You've got a great look. Hair's good, too. That color always comes across great on camera."

Samantha laughed and shook her head. "I've never been on television in my life," she said.

"So?" Robbie shrugged. "You think anybody else here has? Tell you what. Sign up to do makeup and stuff, but give the host job a shot, too."

"I'd be terrible," Samantha protested.

"Maybe," Robbie agreed. "So then you do makeup, right? What have you got to lose?"

Samantha glanced up at Dylan, who was still watching her. She knew she'd never be selected as one of the hosts, but if she tried out, it might be a way to get closer to Dylan Tager. He might not be very quick, but then again, he might just be shy and thoughtful.

"You're right," she said to Robbie. "What have I got to lose?"

 **3**

Karen Jacobs' heart flipped when she walked out of the AV room. Ben was waiting for her, studying some notes. It didn't matter that they'd been going together for a while now. Every time she saw Ben, Karen felt a thrill course through her.

"Hi," she said, walking up to him. "Sorry I took so long. It was a madhouse in there."

Ben closed his notebook. "I know. I was going to come in and wait with you, but I couldn't get through the door." He kissed her softly before they headed down the hall. "So how'd it go?" he asked as they walked along. "Are the cameras ready to roll?"

"Not quite." Karen told him about DeeDee and Robbie. "Robbie is going to drive DeeDee right up the wall," she predicted. "But I think he knows what he's talking about. Television isn't the same as print. I just hope they don't strangle each other."

Ben grinned. "So, when did you sign up to audition for the host job?" he asked.

Karen felt her face flush. She'd signed up because Ben had asked her to, but she was dreading the audition. She knew she'd be just awful. "Tomorrow, during my free period," she told Ben. "They've spaced out the first auditions over the whole day. I'm terrified."

"You'll be great," Ben assured her. "I'm going to love seeing you on TV."

"Ben!" she protested. "I'll never get it. A whole bunch of girls are trying out." At least Emily Van Patten, Ben's beautiful former girlfriend, didn't want to be one of the hosts. Karen liked Emily, but still, being beaten out by her would be humiliating. "Anyway," she added, "I'm going to write for the show. That's what I really want to do." Unfortunately, so did Emily. And Emily was a good writer. Her play was going to be put on by the Drama Club in an evening of one-act plays. She wasn't exactly looking forward to working on the show with Emily, but there wasn't much she could do about it.

"Maybe you'll wind up writing *and* hosting," Ben said.

Karen shook her head, but inside she was

thrilled at how special Ben thought she was. She had to stop feeling inferior to Emily.

As they left the school building, Karen saw Terry coming out a side door. "I just remembered," Karen said to Ben, "that Terry had to stay late to talk to her teacher about a big research project. She's probably walking home. Do you mind if we give her a ride?"

"No, but we're meeting Kevin and Ellen at Leon's, remember? Do you want to ask Terry to come?"

Karen nodded. "Good idea. You get the car and I'll get Terry." She hurried off to catch up with her friend. Ben was so thoughtful.

"Terry?" she called. "Terry, wait up!"

Terry turned and waved, then started walking toward Karen. "Hi," she said. "What's up?"

"I just came from the meeting about the television show," Karen said breathlessly. "You wouldn't believe how many people showed up. Anyway, Ben and I are going to meet Ellen and Kevin over at Leon's. Why don't you come with us?"

Terry's smile faded.

"What's wrong?" Karen asked.

Terry shook her head. "Nothing."

"Well, come on, then," Karen said. "It'll be fun. Aren't you hungry?"

"No . . ." Terry's voice trailed away.

"So come with us, anyway, and get a soda," Karen said.

"Sorry, I can't," Terry said.

Karen laughed. "Oh, come on, I've got a lot of homework, too."

"It's not that. I'm meeting a guy," Terry blurted out.

Karen stared at her friend in surprise. "You *are?* Really?" She grinned. "Wait, I didn't mean it that way. But really?"

Terry nodded, a blush spreading across her face.

Karen's grin got even bigger. "That's great, Terry!" she practically squealed.

"Yeah, well—" Terry glanced at her watch. "Gosh, is it that late? I'd better hurry!"

"Terry!" Karen shrieked. "At least tell me his name!"

"Mickey," Terry said before hurrying off and leaving Karen staring after her.

On Wednesday morning Terry arrived at school just as the final bell rang. Good, she thought. Perfect timing. She could hang back and be the last one inside. That way, if Karen spotted her, there wouldn't be any time for them to talk. Of course she had no idea what she'd do for the rest of the day. Or the next day, or the day after that. How could she explain that her story about having to meet a guy the day before was a total lie? How could she come right out and say that she was so sick and tired of hearing about Karen and Ellen and their boyfriends that she'd made one up for herself?

Thank goodness her parents had been out last night, and her sister Vicki was away at college. The phone had rung twice, and Terry knew one of the callers must have been Karen, wanting to know more about Mickey. She hadn't answered, of course. Now, hurrying down the hall toward homeroom, Terry kept looking over her shoulder, afraid that Karen was going to pop up any second to start grilling her. But she got lucky and made it to class without anyone seeing her. As Terry sank into her seat, she breathed a sigh of relief.

"Hi, you sneak!"

Terry jumped about a foot. Of course. How could she have forgotten? Ellen was in her homeroom, and there she was, a big smile on her face.

"Karen told me," Ellen said, slipping into the next desk. "Mickey, right?"

Terry smiled weakly. Mickey, ha! The only reason she'd called him Mickey was because she happened to be staring at her watch when Karen asked his name, and there was Mickey Mouse, his white-gloved hands pointing out the time. Things could have been worse,

Terry thought glumly. She could have been wearing her Gumby watch.

"So tell me more," Ellen demanded eagerly. "What's Mickey's last name? Does he go here? When did you meet him and how long have you been keeping him a secret from us?"

Just then the homeroom teacher walked in and began taking roll. Thank goodness that's over for now, Terry thought. Maybe by lunch, she'd have the courage to tell her friends the truth.

When lunchtime came, Terry waited until there were only ten minutes left before she headed into the cafeteria. If she was going to confess to being a liar, she didn't want to do it at the beginning of lunch and then sit there while Karen and Ellen felt sorry for her. She didn't think she could stand that.

Terry's stomach was in knots, so she just bought an apple and some milk. Steeling herself, she walked toward the table where Karen and Ellen were waiting. They were both watching her, their eyes bright with anticipation. Terry felt as if she were walking the plank.

"Finally," Karen said as Terry slid into a chair. "Ben and Kevin both had to go to the library, so we can talk. And we're dying to know about Mickey. Tell us absolutely everything."

"Right," Ellen said. "Don't leave out a single detail."

Terry took a deep breath and opened her mouth to reply. But instead of the truth, she heard herself saying, "His name's Mickey Shaw."

"And?" Karen was leaning forward eagerly, her elbows on the table.

Terry couldn't bring herself to tell them the truth. Not yet, anyway. "Well," she said slowly, "he goes to Southside High." That was pretty safe. Southside was a big school, and Karen and Ellen didn't know that many kids who went there.

"Why didn't you tell us about him sooner?" Karen asked. She looked a little hurt.

"I just met him," Terry said. "A week ago."

"How?" Ellen asked.

"Oh—" Good question, Terry thought. "Well, you know, it was just one of those things. We kind of ran into each other. In fact," she went on, warming up a little, "we literally bumped into each other. At the mall. We were coming around a corner from opposite directions and *wham!* I dropped my shopping bag and he picked it up. One thing led to another, and—" She shrugged. "What can I say?" What more *could* she say? Terry took a big bite of her apple, giving herself time to think.

"Okay, now for the good stuff," Ellen said. "What does he look like?"

Terry took a bite of her apple, thinking fast. As long as she'd gone this far, she might as well go all the way and give herself the boy of her dreams. "He's got dark hair," she said. "Really dark, almost black. And blue eyes. Almost gray, you know?"

"Ooh, he sounds gorgeous!" Karen said.

"What else?" Ellen asked. "What's Mickey like?"

"Well, he's kind of shy," Terry said. "But he's not a geek or anything," she added quickly.

"Of course not," Karen said.

"Right," Terry agreed. "Anyway, we started talking, and before I knew it, we'd decided to go to the movies. Then he took me home and, well——"

"Well, what?" Karen said. "Did he kiss you?"

"He sure did!" Terry felt herself blushing, but she figured it probably made her story more convincing. "It was—unbelievable." That, at least, was the truth.

"I'm really happy for you, Terry," Ellen said.

"Me, too," Karen put in.

"Thanks." Terry took another bite of apple and stared at the clock on the cafeteria wall. Only one minute to class. She was saved.

Still chewing, Terry stood up and pointed to the clock. Karen and Ellen got up, too, and the three of them headed across the cafeteria to return their trays.

"So when do we get to meet Mickey?" Karen asked.

Terry swallowed hard. She should have known this was coming. "Um—well, he works after school and—"

"Where?"

"Video City." It was the first place to pop into Terry's mind. But she decided it was a pretty good choice. Video City was huge, with a big staff, and she knew Karen and Ellen usually went to the video store in the mall because it was closer. "His schedule's kind of crazy," she added. "It's even hard for *us* to get together."

Karen nodded knowingly. "I get it. You want to keep him to yourself for a while."

"Sort of," Terry said.

"That's okay, I understand," Karen told her. "I was the same way when Ben and I started going out. I wanted to spend every minute alone with him."

"Right," Terry said.

"Well, we're dying to meet this guy." Ellen slid her tray in the tray return and grinned at Terry. "You can't hide him forever, you know."

As the three of them walked off toward

different classes, Terry let out a deep breath. Then, in spite of everything, she found herself smiling. It was too bad Mickey Shaw didn't exist. She could really fall for a guy like that.

"Okay, Sammy. Just relax and be yourself," Robbie Bodeen said. "I'm not looking for any acting here. I want the real you."

Standing on her mark, a strip of adhesive tape on the floor of the AV room, Samantha gritted her teeth. She hated being called Sammy, especially by someone as obnoxious as Robbie Bodeen. But she had to be nice. "Don't worry, Robbie," she said jokingly. "You'll get the real me, all right. I'm the worst actress in the world."

As Robbie fiddled with the camera, Samantha stifled a yawn. He didn't need to tell her to relax. She wasn't taking her audition very seriously, so she wasn't the least bit nervous.

She'd meant to tell Brittany about the whole thing earlier in the day, but Brittany had been so jumpy about her own audition that Samantha had steered clear of her. Besides, she didn't think Brittany would appreciate knowing that Samantha was auditioning, too. It was ridiculous, of course, because Samantha didn't stand a chance. She wasn't even interested, not really.

Robbie made another minor adjustment to the camera. Then he cocked a finger at Alan Gold, a sophomore. Alan stepped in front of Samantha and held out a clapboard. Samantha couldn't help laughing. This was unreal.

"Okay, all set," Robbie said. "When I give you the sign, Sammy, just start talking about yourself. Tell me what you like, what you don't like, who your friends are, your favorite band, stuff like that. Pretend you're talking to me. But don't look at me, look at the camera, got it?"

"Got it," Samantha said.

"Ready, and—action," Robbie said.

Alan announced Samantha's name and did his thing with the clapboard. Robbie pointed a finger. Samantha faced the camera and smiled. "Hi," she said cheerfully. "I'm Samantha Daley. I'm a junior. I've got kind of reddish brown curly hair. Well, I guess you know that." She paused and tilted her head. "Here's something you don't know, though," she added in confidence—as if the camera lens were a real person. "This is just between you and me, now, so you have to promise not to say a word."

Samantha paused again. She thought she heard Robbie chuckle softly.

"Are you ready for the big secret?" Samantha went on. She lowered her voice slightly. "I have absolutely no idea what I'm doing in front of this camera. I hope it doesn't show, because it sure is fun."

This time, Robbie *did* chuckle, Samantha was sure of it. She hoped he wasn't laughing *at* her, because she'd meant what she'd said. Being on camera really *was* a lot of fun.

 **4**

"Brittany, hi!" Matt Schiller, a dark-haired, athletic senior, put a hand on Brittany's shoulder and spun her around to face him. "Where's the fire?"

Brittany blinked. "Fire? Oh." She managed a smile, even though her mind was still racing. "I'm sorry, Matt. I was hurrying to get to the *Record* office. DeeDee wanted my column for next week this morning, before class." And, Brittany added silently, she wanted to pump DeeDee about the auditions from the day before. DeeDee hadn't actually been around for hers, but she must have seen the tapes by now.

"Listen, I thought we might get together one of these days," Matt said with an easy smile. "See a movie, take a drive."

At last! Brittany had been flirting with

Matt like crazy, and he'd finally taken the bait. Matt already had a girlfriend, but Brittany knew it wasn't serious. He was fair game. Brittany's old boyfriend, Chip Worthington, was hanging out with that simpering Missy Henderson now. So she was free, too.

Brittany put a hand on Matt's arm. "I'd love that, Matt," she said softly.

"Great." Matt flashed a sexy smile. "I've got a lot of workouts this week to get in shape for my next meet, but I'll give you a call as soon as I'm free."

"Perfect," Brittany said, giving his arm a squeeze. "Just don't forget me."

"Not a chance."

"Good," Brittany purred. "I can't wait." Giving Matt's arm another squeeze, Brittany turned and rushed toward the *Record* office. She was glad her column was finished early. Usually she handed it in at the last minute, so this should put DeeDee in a good mood. Maybe it would be easier for Brittany to weasel information out of her.

Brittany knew she'd had a good audition. She'd dressed perfectly—not too alluring, but not boring, either—in a silky, pale coral blouse and black velvet jeans. She'd even gotten up early in the morning to watch the news shows on television and get some ideas about how the women smiled and sat and moved their hands. When Robbie had given her the signal, she was completely prepared. No one could have done better, she was sure of it. In fact, she could already have the job. Maybe when she walked into the *Record* office, DeeDee would congratulate her!

When Brittany walked into the room, though, DeeDee was coughing too hard to say anything. Karen Jacobs was there, patting her on the back.

"What's wrong?" Brittany asked Karen.

"I don't know. She just started coughing." Karen patted DeeDee on the back again. "Are you going to be all right?" she asked.

DeeDee coughed one last time, then took a shaky breath. "I guess so," she said. "I don't know what it is. I woke up this morning feeling awful. Must be a cold." She cleared her throat. "Okay, I'm fine now. Brittany, did you bring your column?"

"Right here," Brittany said, pulling it out of her notebook.

DeeDee took the paper and read it through quickly. "Yeah, looks good, Brittany. Thanks." She handed the column to Karen, who took it to her desk.

"Well!" Brittany said brightly. "Any word on 'Fast Takes'?"

DeeDee frowned. "What a name. You know what Robbie wants to do now? He wants the title shot to be a pair of sneakers going in the main door, and down the hall into the studio. He kept talking about something called chroma-key." She shook her head. "Robbie just wants to play with video toys."

"Oh, well, I'm sure you two will work things out." Brittany thought Robbie's idea was cute, but she wasn't about to say so. "Anyway, what about the hosts? Are you and Robbie arguing about them, too?"

DeeDee smiled wryly. "We haven't picked the girl yet, if that's what you're asking, Brittany."

"Oh." Okay, Brittany thought, so she didn't get it on the first try. "But you must have narrowed down the field, right?"

"Yep." DeeDee sat down at her desk and started making notes to herself. "There are five girls we want to see again, but we're keeping the names quiet. We're just going to tell each of the girls." She shot a warning look at Brittany. "Don't ask me who they are. I'm not telling you, and that's final."

"Well, I know *I'm* not one of them," Karen said with a laugh. "I took one look at the camera and froze."

"You weren't bad," DeeDee told her. "Really, you weren't as bad as some of the others."

"Gee, thanks. But I'm not one of the five, am I?" Karen asked.

DeeDee shook her head. "No, I'm sorry. I'm glad you're writing for the show, though. You'll be good at that."

"Thanks," Karen said again. "That's all I really wanted to do, anyway."

By now, Brittany was almost dancing with impatience. Was DeeDee teasing her, or was it possible that Brittany wasn't one of the five finalists?

"I can tell you two who the guy's going to be," DeeDee said. "Nobody was anywhere near as good as Dylan Tager." She reached for a tissue from the box on her desk and blew her nose. "I can't figure that guy out. I was talking to him before the audition, and I could have sworn he had air where his brain's supposed to be. But the minute he was on camera, he changed completely. He actually sounded intelligent."

"Charisma, I guess," Karen said.

DeeDee nodded. "That was one thing Robbie and I didn't have to fight about." She looked at her watch. "Uh-oh, it's almost time for class. We'd better get going."

"DeeDee!" Brittany almost screamed in frustration.

The editor-in-chief raised her eyebrows. "What, Brittany?" she asked.

"Do you want me to beg? Okay, I'll beg," Brittany said. "Am I one of the five finalists?"

"Oh. Well—" DeeDee suddenly started coughing again. Brittany watched her, unmoved, until DeeDee finally managed to choke out an answer. "Yes. You're one of them, Brittany. Congratulations."

Brittany gave DeeDee a brilliant smile and patted her on the back. "Don't move, DeeDee. I'll get you some water."

At lunchtime Brittany stowed her books in her locker and headed for the AV room. She had to work at her mom's shop, Blooms, again after school, so she'd asked to do her second audition during her lunch period. After DeeDee had stopped coughing, she'd agreed. She thought Dylan McGee would be free then, too. DeeDee and Robbie wanted to see each of the five girls with him.

As she walked down the hall, Brittany realized her stomach was fluttering nervously. It was ridiculous, of course. She didn't know who the other finalists were, but they couldn't possibly be any better than she was. She had the job locked up. Naturally, she'd tried to find out about the other finalists, but DeeDee had refused to say a word.

Before she went to the AV room, Brittany ducked into a bathroom to brush her hair. It would only take a few seconds, and it was important. Good looks were half the battle in TV or any business.

* * *

Just as Brittany disappeared into the bathroom, Samantha came around a near corner and almost bumped into Robbie Bodeen. "Hey, Sammy," he said. "Glad I finally found you. I've been looking all over for you."

"You have?" Samantha said.

"DeeDee didn't catch you, so she asked me to find you," Robbie said.

Samantha shook her head, a little mystified.

"You did great yesterday. You know that, don't you?" Robbie bounced up and down on his feet.

"I did?" Samantha shrugged. "Well, thanks, Robbie. It was fun."

"Yeah, that's what we liked," he said. "You were having a good time, and we could tell. It came across great."

"Thanks," Samantha said again. "So why did you want to see me?"

Robbie leaned close and lowered his voice. "You know we've picked five girls as finalists," he almost whispered. "And you're one of them."

Samantha was speechless.

Robbie grinned. "I knew you'd be excited," he said. "And no kidding, you were good—no really, great. Fantastic southern accent. So listen," he continued, "we're having final auditions today with Dylan Tager. He's our male host."

Samantha nodded. Brittany had told her that between classes. She'd also told her that she was one of the finalists.

"Can you make it right after school?" Robbie asked.

"Sure," Samantha found herself saying. Then she frowned. "This isn't a joke, is it?"

"No joke, Sammy," Robbie assured her. "See you after school at the AV room."

Samantha nodded again and watched him hurry off down the hall. Then, still feeling shell-shocked, she turned and went into the bathroom.

Brittany was standing in front of the mirror.

"Hi," Brittany said, sticking her brush back into her purse. "My hair's not right, is it? I should have worn it in a French braid, but it takes too long to do."

"You look fine," Samantha said. Her own hair was kind of matted to her head—she'd just come from taking a shower after gym. She'd forgotten a shower cap.

"You heard, didn't you? About the five finalists?" Brittany took out a tube of lipstick.

"Yes, you told me earlier, remember?" Samantha said.

"Oh right, I forgot," Brittany said. "I guess I'm kind of excited. I'm on my way to the AV room now." Leaning close to the mirror, Brittany applied a light coat of Tahitian Sunset. Then she capped the tube and stepped back from the mirror to survey her reflection. "I'm glad I changed my mind about wearing my new sweater."

"Oh?" Samantha said weakly.

"It's blazing red. Later, I can wear wild colors on camera once in a while," Brittany went on. "But this royal blue is better for the audition, don't you think?"

"Definitely," Samantha agreed.

Brittany laughed. "That's right—you're doing wardrobe." She took one last look at herself and then headed for the door. "Here goes," she said. "I'll try to call you later and tell you how it went." Waving her fingers at Samantha, she swept out the door.

When the door swung shut, Samantha turned back to the mirror. "You could be in trouble," she said to her reflection. "Big, big trouble."

When Brittany found out that she, Samantha, was one of the other five finalists, she'd probably kill her.

Still, Samantha couldn't help feeling a little thrill. She'd gone to the audition the day before not even wanting the job. But once she'd started talking to the camera, she'd discovered how easy it was! And now she had been called back!

Taking out her own brush, Samantha

started working on her hair. It would be fine by the end of the day, when she had to audition again.

True, Brittany would be furious if she found out, but maybe she'd never know. Samantha definitely wouldn't tell a soul.

Of course, Samantha could forget the whole thing and just not show up. But she'd discovered something that nobody knew—she wanted that job. Why shouldn't she go after it? It would be much more exciting than doing makeup and wardrobe, and it would look great on her record, too.

The day before she'd treated the whole thing as a joke, and when she went in to the audition after school, she'd still be smiling. Inside, though, Samantha Daley would be deadly serious.

In the AV room, Brittany took a few deep breaths to relax herself. She'd read somewhere that that was supposed to help. Of course, she didn't want to take too many deep breaths, or she might hyperventilate.

Robbie and his technical whiz, Alan, were conferring about sound. Dylan Tager was sitting in the chair next to Brittany. She wanted to talk to him, but he was staring off into space so hard, she thought he must be concentrating on something important.

"Okay, listen up," Robbie said at last. "DeeDee can't be here, but let's get started.

Dyl, you've done this once already so you know the routine, right?''

Dylan brought his fingers to his forehead in a mock salute, then smiled at Brittany. Brittany beamed at him. Taping a show with him would be pure pleasure.

''Good man,'' Robbie said. ''Now, listen, Brit. Today I want you to do some chitchat with Dylan. He'll start out saying something about that new trig teacher, what's-her-name.''

''Miss Tedesco,'' Dylan said.

''Right.''

''I don't know her,'' Brittany said, fighting down a panicky feeling.

''Don't worry about it,'' Robbie told her. ''Dylan doesn't, either. DeeDee gave him all the info he needs. So he'll start talking and you'll ask questions, get it?''

Brittany nodded. ''Yes, I get it.''

''Good. So, you two do a little back and forth until I say cut,'' Robbie went on. ''We just want to see how the two of you work together. The chemistry's important.''

Brittany gave Dylan one of her sultriest smiles. He slowly grinned back, and Brittany felt a twinge of triumph. The chemistry was going to be no problem at all.

5

"Tell me more," Karen urged Terry. "All I've heard so far is that Mickey's gorgeous and a little shy."

It was the last period of the day, and the two of them were in the school library, doing research on the Italian Renaissance. Encyclopedias couldn't be checked out, so they were waiting to use the copy machine, both of them loaded down with the heavy books.

Fortunately, Terry had spent some time after lunch thinking up more details about her fictitious new boyfriend, so she was prepared. "Well, he loves old movies, just like me," she said. "In fact, I'm meeting him at Video City after school today and we're going to pick one out to watch together tomorrow night. He works until nine on

Fridays, so that's what we usually do." She suddenly remembered that she'd said she and Mickey had only known each other for a week. "I mean," she added quickly, "that's what we've *decided* we'll do."

"Sounds like fun," Karen said.

Terry nodded. "Let's see, what else? He's got an old Mustang convertible that he works on every free minute he gets."

"I bet he won't spend as much time on it now that he's got you," Karen said.

"Oh, well, of course." Terry laughed. "It is a great car, though. Mickey just finished painting it. Candy apple red."

They were at the copy machine now. Karen held the books while Terry ran the machine. "Did I tell you Mickey likes J. D. Salinger?" Terry went on.

"You're kidding," Karen said. "He's your favorite, right?"

"Right," Terry said. "And he's thinking about studying medicine. But he doesn't want to specialize and get rich doing surgery or anything like that. He thinks the country needs more family doctors, especially in poor areas."

Karen shook her head, amazed. "He sounds perfect."

Terry was ready for this, too. "Oh, he's got a few flaws. He likes to cook."

Karen stared at her. "What's wrong with that?"

Terry giggled. "He's terrible. He thinks he's some kind of gourmet chef, but the other night he made pizza and the dough was like rubber."

"That doesn't sound like much of a fault, though," Karen said, handing Terry the last book. "At least he tried."

"Oh, sure," Terry agreed. "But I hope he'll stick with cheeseburgers from now on." She flipped the book shut and handed it back to Karen, then gathered up all the copies. As they headed to a table to sort them, Terry decided to change the subject. It was fun, making up things about her almost-perfect boyfriend, but she had to stop herself. She was going to have to confess one of these days, and the more lies she told, the harder it would be to come clean.

Or maybe she wouldn't confess, Terry thought suddenly. Maybe she should just wait a couple of days and then tell Karen and Ellen that she and Mickey had broken up. That might be the best way out.

"You're not upset about not getting the host part, are you?" Terry asked Karen. "You've been kind of quiet."

"No, I'm just thinking about Emily," Karen said, a little sigh escaping from her lips. "She's going to be writing for the show, too, you know. It seems that I can't escape that girl, no matter what."

Terry was curious. "I thought you were starting to like her."

"I am," Karen said. "But I don't think I'll ever be really comfortable with her. Every time I see her, I can't help being afraid that Ben will decide to go back to her."

"That's crazy," Terry told her. "Ben loves you. It's over with Emily."

"That's what I keep telling myself." Karen sighed. "I don't suppose Mickey has a beautiful girlfriend in his past, does he?"

Terry wasn't ready for that. She accidentally knocked a sheet off the table, giving herself time to think while she picked it up. "Well, he's had a girlfriend or two," she said. "But no big love of his life, I guess."

Karen smiled weakly, and the two of them began reshelving the encyclopedias. When the bell rang, Karen said, "I've got my mom's car. Do you want a ride?"

"Sure, that'd be great," Terry said.

After picking up their schoolbooks and coats, they walked outside to the student parking lot.

"This is luxury," Terry said as she got into the passenger seat. "I get so sick of riding the bus."

"Mmm." Karen grinned mischievously as she backed out of the parking spot. "Actually, I had an ulterior motive."

Terry frowned. "What's that?"

"You said you are meeting Mickey at Video City, right?" Karen asked. "I'll take you there. This is the perfect chance for me to check him out."

As Karen pulled out of the parking lot, Terry closed her eyes and slid down in her seat, feeling slightly sick. Unless Video City had burned down during the night, she was trapped.

"Okay, Dylan!" Robbie said. "Last audition. Are you up for it?"

Dylan stifled a yawn and nodded. "I think I could do it in my sleep," he said, bored.

Samantha cocked her head. As far as she was concerned, Dylan was already asleep. She'd tried to make conversation with him while they were waiting for Robbie to set up the camera, but she'd gotten nowhere. She could have flirted with him, but that took too much energy, and she didn't want to waste any before the audition. Maybe later, she thought. Then she'd turn on the charm and see if he was worth going after. She wanted to start dating somebody, if for no reason other than to show Kyle that she wasn't completely torn up over him. Of course, she *was* still hurt—and she missed Kyle. Dylan was great looking, but if he turned out to be a dimwit, Samantha didn't think she could stand him. Not after Kyle, who was both smart and funny.

"All right, let's do it," Robbie said. "Sammy, you take your cue from Dylan. He'll be talking about the new trig teacher, and you just say whatever comes to mind. You all set?"

Samantha nodded and sat up a little straighter in her chair. Dylan smoothed back his hair and cleared his throat. Robbie checked with Alan, who was running the tape deck, and then called, "Action."

"Hi," Dylan said into the camera. "Welcome to 'Fast Takes.' We've got a lot on the platter today, starting with River Heights High's newest teacher. Her name's June Tedesco, and she teaches trigonometry." He turned to Samantha and smiled. "Who said women weren't good at math?"

Samantha stared at him for a second. It was amazing the way Dylan had suddenly come to life, like a wind-up toy. But his remark about women and math was something she couldn't ignore. "Well, *I* certainly never said it, Dylan," she told him. "And I wouldn't believe it for a minute."

"I'm sure you're right." Dylan nodded, his golden eyes bright with warmth. "You're from the South, aren't you, Samantha?"

"I sure am," Samantha said, making her accent even stronger.

"Well, so is Ms. Tedesco," Dylan said. "Beaufort, South Carolina, in fact."

"Really?" Samantha said, genuinely surprised. "I've got an uncle in Beaufort. I wonder if she knows him."

"Maybe you can ask her," Dylan said. "It's time to go to the interview right now." He turned away from Samantha and into the camera.

"Okay, cut," Robbie said. "That's it. Nice work. I like the part about the uncle, Sammy. Nice touch."

Dylan stood up. "Well, good luck," he said.

"Thanks," Samantha said. She was glad Robbie thought she'd done well. It was too bad there wasn't anybody she could talk to about it.

As she left the building, Samantha saw Kyle and Sasha strolling across the quad toward the parking lot. Sasha was carrying a big, rolled-up piece of paper under one arm. Probably an art project, Samantha thought. Kyle was holding her other hand, and they were laughing. Well, she couldn't talk to Kyle about the audition, that was for sure. He wouldn't care, anyway. He and Samantha were quits.

Samantha walked slowly, not wanting to run into them in the parking lot. When she saw Kyle's hideous pickup back out of a spot, she sped up, hurrying toward her mother's car, which she'd borrowed for the day.

As she reached it, she saw Kim and Jeremy and Jeremy's buddies, Hal Evans and Wayne Yale, standing next to Jeremy's Porsche.

"I thought you already left," Kim called out.

"I needed some help with an assignment," Samantha lied. Well, it wasn't a total lie. She could always use help with one assignment or another. "Where are you all off to?" she asked, walking over to them.

"The club," Jeremy said.

"The country club?"

"Is there any other club worth going to?" Hal asked. He and Wayne snickered.

Samantha shot them a dirty look. They were so obnoxious, she didn't know how Kim could stand having them around.

Kim put her arm through Jeremy's. "Do you want to come with us?" she asked Samantha.

"Yeah," Wayne said. "You can ride with Hal and me."

Samantha suppressed a shudder. "No, thanks," she said. "I think I'll just go home."

"Boring," Jeremy remarked.

Kim poked him in the ribs and then walked over to Samantha, pulling her apart from the others. "Why don't you come?" she asked. "You don't have to ride with Hal and Wayne. Look, I can tell you're still feeling down about Kyle. Maybe if you come to the club, it'll take your mind off him."

Samantha was tempted, but she was afraid she'd let something slip about the audition, and telling Kim was as good as telling Brittany. She could make Kim promise not to tell, of course, but it was safer not to take the chance. "Thanks," she said to Kim. "But I really should get on home. I've got a ton of homework."

"Well, okay," Kim said. "If you change your mind, you know where we'll be."

Feeling a little lonely, Samantha got in her car and headed home. If she did get the host job, she knew she'd have to deal with Brittany. But it would be worth it, she decided. Without Kyle, there was an empty spot in her life, and the host job might be a way to fill it up.

Fortunately, it was a fifteen-minute drive to Video City, so Terry had some time to pull herself together. As Karen pulled into the crowded parking lot, Terry said, "Hey, this is great. I can't wait for you to meet Mickey." She was trying to sound excited, but then she looked at her watch. "Oh, no!" she exclaimed, faking disappointment. "I just realized something."

"What?" Karen asked.

"Mickey doesn't start work for another half hour," Terry told her.

Karen shrugged. "No problem, I can wait. Maybe I'll reserve a tape for the weekend."

"Oh. Sure." Terry tried not to panic. If she panicked, she wouldn't be able to think. She started to open the door. "Uh-oh," she said, slapping herself on the forehead. "I just remembered something else. Mickey told me last night that he was going to be starting even later today. He had to go to a meeting of the—the film club at his school."

"He's into film?" Karen asked. "You didn't tell me that."

"Didn't I?" Terry tried to smile. "I guess I forgot. He wants to take film classes in college."

Karen frowned. "I thought he wanted to be a doctor."

"Oh, he does! He just wants to study film on the side because he loves it so much." Terry forced a laugh. "So, anyway, I guess you wouldn't want to hang out here for a whole hour." She crossed her fingers.

"No, I guess you're right," Karen said. "I'd better get home. You don't mind waiting an hour for him, of course," she added teasingly.

Thank goodness, Terry thought. She was off the hook. "Are you kidding?" she said as she hurried out of the car before Karen could change her mind. "I'd wait forever for Mickey!"

Which is exactly what she'd have to do, she thought grimly, pushing open the door of Video City.

Inside the store, Terry wandered around aimlessly. She didn't really want a tape, but as long as she was there, she might as well get one. Her homework that night was pretty light, and what else did she have to do once she'd finished it?

She was still wandering, feeling sorry for herself, when a voice startled her.

"Are you looking for something in particular?"

Terry glanced at him. She could tell he worked in the store because of his Video City name tag, which said, "Brian."

"Old movies," Terry said.

Brian shrugged. "Right over there," he said, pointing to a sign that read Classics.

"Thanks." Terry left him and went over to the tapes. She'd seen *Casablanca* lots of times, but not lately. Besides, it would make her cry, and she felt like doing that.

Terry brought the tape to the counter. Brian took her money. "You like old movies, huh?" he asked. He sounded as if he couldn't understand why anyone would.

"Yes," Terry said curtly. Who was he to judge, anyway?

"Oh, well." Brian gave her the tape and her change. "Enjoy it."

"Thanks." Terry turned away and left the store. A light rain had started, which got heavier as she walked two blocks to the bus stop. She hoped the bus would hurry. It was starting to get dark, and the rain was cold and turning to sleet.

She pulled up the hood on her down coat and shivered.

Hunching her shoulders against the cold, Terry closed her eyes and thought of Mickey. Maybe he wasn't real, but at the moment, fantasy was better than reality. Did he like sports? Yes, but he wasn't a total jock. He liked shooting baskets in his driveway, and he ran on the cross-country track team. What about music? He liked rock and big bands, too, like Terry did. He had a great sense of humor, and he didn't mind laughing at himself.

Spinning out the fantasy, Terry hardly felt the cold and sleet. When the next car slowly drove by, she was almost surprised that it wasn't Mickey's bright red Mustang.

6

Brittany looked at her watch for the fifteenth time in the past three minutes. Six-thirty. DeeDee had to have seen the audition tapes by now. Robbie had said he was going to drive them to her house right after school. If her mother's shop wasn't so busy at the moment, Brittany could have tried to call DeeDee at least. Instead, she was so busy writing up orders and helping people pick out flower arrangements that she hadn't even had time to eat the apple she'd brought for a snack.

Drumming her fingers impatiently, Brittany watched her latest customer slowly turn the pages of the catalog.

"It's for my mother," the woman said to Brittany. "She's in the hospital. Nothing serious, thank goodness."

"Mmm," Brittany said. How could she hurry this woman along? "Well, how about this one?" She took the book and flipped quickly through the pages. "Flowers and candy," she suggested, pointing at one of the pictures. "And a little balloon, see? It says 'Get Well Soon.' It's one of our biggest sellers," she added pointedly. If the woman would just agree, Brittany might have time to write up the order before another customer came in, and then call DeeDee.

"Well, it's nice," the woman said doubtfully. "But I'm not sure about the candy. My mother's diabetic."

She reached for the book, but before she could get her hands on it, Brittany slapped a couple of more pages over. "Flowers and fruit," she said triumphantly. "Perfect."

"Very nice," the woman agreed. "But she lives in Florida. She's surrounded by fruit trees."

Brittany gritted her teeth. "You can never have too much fruit," she said.

"I suppose you're right." The woman smiled. "All right, I'll take this one."

Brittany whipped out an order form and got all the information she needed before the woman could change her mind. Finally the store was empty, except for her mother, who was in the back room making up arrangements for a wedding party. Brittany picked up the phone and punched in DeeDee's number.

Busy.

Now what? She could call again when she got home, but she was dying to find out right then, that very minute. Maybe DeeDee's line was busy because she was trying to call Brittany and tell her she'd gotten the job.

Brittany tried DeeDee's number again. Still busy. Frustrated, she slammed the phone down and leaned on the counter, staring through the window at the people passing by in the mall.

Suddenly she squinted and straightened up again. Was that Robbie Bodeen? Yes, definitely. Robbie was passing by the window, walking fast and bobbing up and down as he always did. If Brittany hurried, she could catch up with him. She couldn't stand the guy—he was much too hyper—but she'd manage to hide her dislike long enough to get an answer out of him.

"Mom!" she called, scooting out from behind the counter and heading for the door. "There aren't any customers right now. I'm going to get a soda. Do you want anything?"

"Thanks, honey. Some juice would be great," her mother called back.

Flinging open the door, Brittany hurried out of the store and down the hall in the direction Robbie had gone, keeping her eyes peeled for the purple sweatshirt he was wearing. There he was, just a few feet in front of her, heading into Platters, the record store.

"Robbie!" Brittany called.

Robbie stopped suddenly and spun around.

"Robbie!" Brittany raised her hand and hurried toward him.

"Hey, Brit," he greeted her.

"Hi," she said a little breathlessly. "I just happened to see you walking by—I work in the flower store back there—so I thought I'd come out and say hello."

"You have a job?" Robbie asked.

Uh-oh. Maybe she shouldn't have said that. Now he might think there'd be a time conflict if she was one of the hosts. "Well, it's my mother's store, and I can pretty much set my own hours," she told him.

Robbie didn't seem interested. His gaze kept darting around the mall. "You know, I came down here to get some tapes," he said. "I've got to find the right theme music for 'Fast Takes.' But now I'm wondering if we should do a segment on this place. You know, teen consumerism or something like that. What do you think?"

"Sounds great," Brittany said. She would have agreed with anything.

"Yeah, I'll run it by DeeDee," Robbie was saying, more to himself than to Brittany. "Who knows? Maybe I'll get lucky and she'll like one of my ideas for a change."

Brittany shifted her weight, trying to hide her impatience. Didn't he know she was dying to find out about the host job? Hoping to sound casual, she asked, "So, how did the audition tapes come out?"

"Huh?" Robbie finally focused on Brittany again. "Oh. Real good. You did a nice job, Brit."

Finally! Brittany's heart pounded in anticipation. "Oh, thank you," she said, smiling modestly. "It was really fun. I think Dylan and I—"

"Yeah, it's going to be a hard choice."

Brittany's mouth got dry. "You mean, you still haven't decided?"

Robbie shook his head. "We've got it narrowed down to two, and you're one of them," he told her. "I talked to DeeDee, and for once we actually see eye to eye." He grinned. "Miracles do happen, I guess. Anyway, it looks like we have to have one more audition, next Wednesday, I think. This one'll be tough—we're going to do a run-through of an actual segment."

Brittany was hardly listening now. The important thing was that she'd made it to the finals!

"DeeDee and I couldn't make up our minds," Robbie went on. "You and Sammy were both great in different ways, you know what I mean? You're smooth and sophisticated, and she's—"

"Sammy?" Brittany interrupted. Who on earth was Sammy?

Robbie grinned. "You know me, I talk fast. Her name's Samantha. Samantha—" He snapped his fingers, trying to recall her last name.

"Daley?" Brittany asked through gritted teeth.

"That's it! How could I forget?" Robbie said. "Sort of reddish brown hair, southern accent, real cute."

"That's her, all right," Brittany said. Her former friend, Samantha Daley.

"Well, listen, I gotta go," Robbie said. "Catch you later, Brit."

Brittany managed a friendly goodbye, then turned and started back to Blooms, her jaw clenched in anger. If she'd seen Samantha at that moment, she would have been tempted to strangle her. How could Samantha have betrayed her like this? Brittany wondered.

Just as Brittany reached Blooms, she heard someone call her name. Turning, she saw Kim and Jeremy walking toward her, hand in hand. Trailing behind them were Hal and Wayne.

"We were on our way home from the club," Kim explained, "and Jeremy wanted to pick up some shirts he'd ordered, so I decided to—" She stopped, peering closely at Brittany. "What's the matter with you? Your face is all red."

"Too much time under the sunlamp?" Jeremy suggested, chuckling at his own humor. Hal and Wayne cackled along with him.

Brittany ignored them. "Did you know about Samantha?" she asked Kim accusingly. "If you knew and didn't tell me—"

"Know what?" Kim broke in. "What are you talking about?"

"'Fast Takes,'" Brittany snapped.

Kim and Jeremy exchanged glances, their eyebrows raised. Kim shrugged. "I don't know what you're talking about, Brittany."

"Samantha tried out for the host spot," Brittany said, practically spitting out the words. "She actually tried out and never told me. And now the choice is between me and her."

"Hey, battle of the network stars," Jeremy said. His two sidekicks laughed again.

"Stuff it, Jeremy," Brittany said. She turned back to Kim. "Can you believe it? Our best friend has stabbed me in the back."

"Look," Kim said, "before you kill Samantha, why don't you talk to her? There's got to be some kind of explanation."

"I'm sure there is," Brittany said icily. "But nothing she says will matter. As far as I'm concerned, she's a back-stabbing traitor."

At that moment the traitor was eating a hearty meal in her dining room and describing her second audition to her parents. "I felt so comfortable," Samantha said, forking up a cucumber slice from her salad. "Since it was the second time around, I guess it just felt natural."

"This is *so* exciting!" her mother said. "Isn't it fabulous, John? Our little girl's going to be famous!"

Mr. Daley nodded vigorously. "I'm proud of you, sugar. We had no idea this is what you were going to do."

"That's right," Mrs. Daley said. "We thought you were just going to work on makeup. We didn't know you'd be the star! Why didn't you tell us?"

Samantha laughed. "I'm not the star yet, Mom. I have a lot of competition. I might not get the job, you know."

"Don't talk like that," her mother warned, waving her fork in the air. "It's bad luck."

"This is going to look very good on your high school record," Mr. Daley said to Samantha. "It shows you're a real go-getter."

Up till then, the only thing Samantha had really been interested in was having fun. She'd always thought getting involved in extracurricular activities would cut into her valuable free time. Being on "Fast Takes" would, too, but it would be worth it. She'd be a celebrity, at least at River Heights High. Not only would it be fun, but Kyle Kirkwood would remember exactly who it was he was missing. There was no way Sasha Lopez could ever be a host on a TV show!

"So, who's ready for dessert?" Mrs. Daley asked, getting up from the table. "I stopped by the bakery this morning and bought a scrumptious peach pie."

Mr. Daley immediately said yes, but Samantha thought she'd better stay away from desserts, at least until she knew whether she had the part or not. She was slender, but she couldn't afford to take a chance on gaining weight, not if she was going to be in front of a camera from now on.

Excusing herself, Samantha carried the dinner plates into the kitchen. She was just getting ready to load the dishwasher when the phone rang. "I'll get it!" she called. Maybe it was Robbie or DeeDee, telling her she'd gotten the part.

It was Kim. "Just a friendly warning," Kim said when Samantha answered. "Brittany's out for your blood."

7

On Friday morning Brittany strode across the quad, her hair tumbling around her shoulders in dark shining waves, her smile as bright as the new yellow sweater she wore under her leather coat. She waved and called greetings to everyone she knew, stopping once or twice to chat for a few seconds. No one would ever have guessed that she was boiling mad inside.

No one except Samantha and Kim, who were standing near the front steps.

"Here she comes," Samantha said, taking a deep breath.

"Nervous?" Kim asked.

"Wouldn't you be?" Samantha said. "Brittany's been furious with you before—you know what it's like. I just want to get this over with. Once I explain how the whole thing happened, she'll understand. Then we can be friendly rivals."

Kim snorted. "Brittany's been competing with everyone since kindergarten, and she's *never* been friendly about it."

Samantha watched as Brittany came closer. "Well, here goes nothing."

When Brittany walked up to them, Samantha stepped a few feet away from Kim, so that she was standing alone. If Brittany noticed her, she gave absolutely no sign of it. With a quick wave and a smile at Kim, Brittany sailed up the steps and through the front doors of River Heights High.

Kim sighed and walked over to Samantha. "Well," she said dryly, "there went nothing."

Once inside the building, Brittany let her mask drop and frowned as she made her way through the halls and up to the *Record* office. The nerve of Samantha Daley! Planting herself out there like a statue, smiling as if they were still friends. After what Samantha had done, trying out for the host job and not even saying a word about it, Brittany couldn't believe she'd had the guts to even show up at school that morning.

She'd get Samantha for this, one way or another. The best way, of course, would be to win the part. She had no idea how Samantha could possibly have gotten this far in the contest, but that was beside the point. Robbie had said it was going to be a close call, and Brittany was ready to do everything in her power to make sure she came out on top.

After pushing open the door to the *Record* office, Brittany walked in and stood in the middle of the room, glaring.

The place was busy. Dave Millwood, a sophomore who wanted to be an investigative journalist, was trying to convince Mr. Greene, the faculty advisor, to let him do a surprise inspection of the cafeteria kitchen. Kathy Russo and Sarah Weiner were typing away on two brand-new computer keyboards. Karen Jacobs was leaning over a table, working on a layout.

"Where's DeeDee?" Brittany called to no one in particular.

"I know I'll uncover something," Dave said to Mr. Greene. "There's got to be a reason why the food's so bad."

"It's institutional food, Dave," Mr. Greene said patiently. "It's never going to rate four stars in any restaurant guide."

"But—"

"Where's DeeDee?" Brittany called again.

"Dave, I'm sorry," Mr. Greene said, nodding to Brittany as he headed for the door, "but you're barking up the wrong tree. The kitchen's open to anyone who wants to go in. What could they be hiding?"

Still arguing, Dave followed the faculty advisor out the door.

"Where's DeeDee?" Brittany shouted.

"Sick," Kathy said, without taking her eyes off her monitor.

Brittany frowned. "Sick? What do you mean, sick?"

"Aches, coughing, fever of a hundred and three," Sarah reported with a shrug. "She says she feels like somebody stomped on her."

"It's the flu," Karen told Brittany. "DeeDee called me this morning."

"My mother just got over it," Sarah said. "DeeDee will be lucky if she's back in a week. My mother was sick for ten days."

"Ten days!" Brittany exclaimed, her heart sinking.

"I know, next week's a busy time for the paper," Karen said. "But we'll manage."

The paper was the last thing on Brittany's mind. The night before, after a few hours of fuming about Samantha's treachery, she'd finally started to think clearly. What Brittany really needed was someone on her side, someone who'd push for her to be the host. DeeDee, of course, was the obvious choice. Brittany just had to remind DeeDee about how she'd always come through for the *Record*. She was sure she could get DeeDee in her corner.

With DeeDee out sick, Brittany was on her own. She didn't think she could influence Robbie Bodeen because all he really knew about her was what he'd seen in the audition. Besides, he was so obnoxious, the thought of flirting with him or buttering him up was revolting. If she got desperate enough, Brittany told herself, she might have to do it. But first, she'd try to think of something else.

At lunch Samantha decided to try one more time to explain things to Brittany. She didn't blame Brittany for being upset, not really. Maybe she'd have to admit that she shouldn't have kept her auditions a secret.

After choosing a salad and a carton of juice, Samantha carried her tray straight to the table where Brittany and Kim were sitting.

"I'll get right to the point, Brittany," she said as she sat down. "You're mad and I don't blame you. When I first auditioned, it was just for kicks. I'm not sure why I even did it, and I honestly didn't think I had a chance. But then I started to *want* the part." Samantha paused, but Brittany didn't say anything, so she went on. "I knew how much you wanted to be the host, too, and I guess I chickened out about telling you. It was a sneaky way to act and I'm sorry." There, she thought. She'd done it.

Kim shifted in her chair and looked back and forth between Brittany and Samantha. "Well, that's over," she said. "Let's eat."

Brittany didn't speak until Samantha had taken her first bite of salad. "Do you really think an apology makes everything all right?" she asked coldly.

Her mouth full, Samantha could only stare at Brittany.

"Well, it doesn't," Brittany went on. "If it weren't for you, that job would be mine. The last thing in the world I expected was for one of my two best *friends* to stand in my way."

Kim cleared her throat. "But, Brittany, she already said she never thought she'd get this far. She didn't really plan it, it just kind of happened."

"Look, Brittany, I really need an activity for my high school record," Samantha said. "I told you that. You already write for the paper, and you want to be editor-in-chief next year when DeeDee leaves. You can't do that and be the host, too."

"Samantha's got a point," Kim said.

Brittany shot her a withering glance. "Whose side are you on?"

"The side of peace," Kim said, waving her spoon with a little flourish.

"Besides," Samantha added, "you know how awful I've felt since Kyle broke up with me. This TV show would really help take my mind off him." She sighed, hoping Brittany would at least feel a little sympathy for her.

Brittany was too angry to care. "What gave you the idea that you were a journalist?" she asked Samantha. "The only newspapers you ever read are the trashy tabloids in the supermarket check-out lines."

Samantha tossed down her napkin. "You're way out of line, Brittany. The hosts of 'Fast Takes' don't have to be journalists—they have to be personalities. Mine just happens to be the right kind of personality."

"Oh?" Brittany raised her eyebrows. "You mean they're looking for sneaky little back-stabbers?"

"Come on, you guys," Kim said. "Why don't you just take it easy? I mean, this is a little friendly competition, not a war."

"It wouldn't be a competition if Samantha hadn't tried out," Brittany said.

"Where do you get off telling me I can't even want the same thing you want?" Samantha asked.

Brittany snorted. "You don't stand a chance, you know," she said. "I'm going to get that job. You might as well give up now before you're totally humiliated."

"I came here and apologized so we could be friends again," Samantha said. She shoved back her chair and stood up. "Now, not only do I take back my apology, but I'm going to go out and win that part. You want a fight, Brittany? You've got one!''

After Samantha stalked away from the table, Kim turned to Brittany. "I was wrong," she said. "It *is* a war."

Still seething, Samantha sped through the halls to her locker. She absolutely could not believe Brittany. Telling her she didn't stand a chance for the host job. Insulting her with remarks about the supermarket tabloids! Samantha had never in her life read a tabloid at the supermarket. At the drugstore, maybe, but never at the supermarket.

The battle lines were drawn now, and Samantha knew Brittany. That girl would stoop to anything to get what she wanted.

As Samantha spun the combination on her locker, she suddenly felt a twinge of nervousness. Brittany *would* do anything to get the job. Who knew what tricks she would try? Samantha had to think of a plan, too, or she might lose.

Staring into her locker, Samantha heard footsteps approaching and the sound of laughter. Lacey Dupree and her new boyfriend, Tom Stratton, had stopped at the water fountain. When Lacey bent over the fountain, Tom gently held her long, red-gold hair back so it wouldn't get wet. Samantha felt a real pang of jealousy and thought of

Kyle. Then she gave herself a mental shake. She *had* to get that host job. Then she'd be too busy to miss Kyle.

Samantha was poking around in her locker, looking for the books she needed, when she realized Tom and Lacey were still behind her, talking. She didn't mean to eavesdrop, but it was almost impossible not to.

"Just think," Lacey was saying, "the dance at Southside tomorrow night is your first gig. It's so great!"

"Yeah," Tom agreed. "I hope it's not our last one."

"Oh, come on," Lacey said. "You guys'll get lots more work."

Samantha remembered now. Tom had a band. She hadn't heard them, but she'd heard they were good.

"We're not the only band in town," Tom told Lacey.

"But Mock Three is the best," Lacey said loyally.

"Thanks," Tom said with a laugh. "You know that and I know that, but nobody else does. I wish there was some way we could get more people to hear about us."

"Right!" Lacey said excitedly. "You need to promote yourselves, like with a radio spot or newspaper ad."

"Those cost money, and none of us are exactly rolling in it," Tom reminded her.

"Besides," he added, "the whole commercial side of bands really turns me off."

"I know, but I'm good at that end of the business," Lacey said. "I was the one who got the Deadbeats to come to River Heights earlier this year."

"That's right," Tom said. "I remember Rick talking about it. Only you could pull off a stunt like that."

Samantha shut her locker and turned around. When Lacey had said "radio," a lightbulb flashed on in Samantha's head. "Hi, you two," she said, walking over to them with a friendly smile. "Don't be mad, now, because I really wasn't trying to listen in. But I couldn't help hearing what you were saying, and I think I've got the answer to your problem."

Tom and Lacey exchanged glances. Samantha wasn't usually friendly. "What do you mean?" Tom asked, frowning.

"Well, you've heard about 'Fast Takes,' right?" Samantha said. "The magazine show?"

"Sure," Tom said, ready to tune out. It was obvious television didn't interest him at all.

"Well, anyway," Samantha said quickly, "when I heard you talking about advertising, I thought, 'Why should they go for radio? We've got a free television studio right here at River Heights High!'"

This time Lacey looked excited. "Of course!" she said to Tom. "If they did a segment on Mock Three for 'Fast Takes,' we could use the tape as a promotion piece."

"You could show it to whoever hires live acts at Commotion," Samantha said. "I bet they'd hire you in a minute—if you're good enough."

"Oh, they're definitely good enough," Lacey said. "What do we have to do?"

Samantha leaned closer and lowered her voice. "I just happen to know one of the producers, Robbie Bodeen," she said. "And I'm almost positive I can get him to Southside tomorrow night." She smiled. "The rest of it would be up to you."

Tom was serious now and very interested. "We wouldn't disappoint him, he can count on that."

"Thanks, Samantha," Lacey said, sounding surprised. "This is really nice of you."

"Oh, don't thank me," Samantha told her. "Really, I'm happy to do it." She waggled her fingers at Tom and Lacey as she walked away, still smiling to herself. All she had to do now was talk Robbie into going with her to Southside the next night. But that shouldn't be hard. She would tell him she'd heard of a hot new band that could really sizzle. Sizzle was exactly what Robbie was looking for, for "Fast Takes."

If everything worked out, Robbie would be grateful to Samantha. So grateful, he might even feel obligated to repay her. And what better way to do that than to choose her, Samantha Daley, as the cohost for "Fast Takes"?

8

"You know, Sammy, I can't let this influence me," Robbie said as they drove in his minivan to Southside High on Saturday night. "I'm dying to produce a rock video, but even if this band turns out to be my ticket to fame, it won't mean a thing when it comes to my decision on the 'Fast Takes' host. I have to choose the best person, whoever it is."

"Of course you do," Samantha said, gripping the armrest as the van rounded a corner. Robbie drove the way he walked—as if he were always ten minutes behind schedule and had to rush.

"I just thought this was something you wouldn't want to miss, that's all," Samantha went on. "And even if I don't get the job, I still want the show to be great." That sounded professional, she thought, even though it wasn't true. If Brittany got the job, Samantha knew she wouldn't be broken-hearted if the show flopped.

"It'll be great," Robbie said, flashing a quick grin. "Count on it. Of course, I have to keep DeeDee from dragging it down. No offense to her, but she just doesn't know video."

"It must be frustrating for you," Samantha said, clutching the armrest for another left turn.

"Yeah, well, we managed to compromise on the segment for next week's audition, at least," Robbie said.

Samantha perked up. "Oh?"

Robbie laughed. "Huh-uh," he said. "Can't tell you what it is, Sammy. No way. You and Brittany will both have to take your chances. It wouldn't be fair if you knew and she didn't, right?"

"Right." Samantha forced herself to laugh, too. She was getting awfully tired of being called Sammy.

"I'll tell you this, though," Robbie said. "The segment's not going to be just chitchat. The hosts will be *doing* something, not just talking to the camera."

"I don't suppose you can give me a hint," Samantha said.

"Sure, why not?" Robbie grinned. "When I say 'cut,' you can take it literally."

Some hint, Samantha thought, completely mystified.

At last Robbie slammed the minivan into the Southside High parking lot and jerked to a stop. Samantha pried her fingers loose from the armrest and got out. Robbie joined her, and they took off for the gym, with Robbie always a good half step ahead.

They heard Mock Three long before they got inside. Tom's band was playing a wild, pulsing number, heavy on the bass and drums. Robbie grabbed Samantha's hand. "Do you like to dance?"

"Sure," Samantha said. She hadn't really planned on dancing, but maybe it would wear him out enough to make the drive home slow and safe. Besides, she had to be nice to him. She was just glad she didn't really know anyone at Southside. She didn't want people to get the idea that she was dating Robbie Bodeen.

The gym was decorated with balloons and streamers of crepe paper in Southside's colors, green and gold. Strobe lights flashed over the crowd, bathing the dancers' faces in streaks of red and green and yellow. The band was on a raised platform at one end, dressed in black jeans and tight T-shirts, with Tom Stratton on lead guitar. When they finished the number, they went right into another one.

Samantha and Robbie danced through

three more numbers until the band finally took a break. Robbie grabbed Samantha's hand to lead her toward the platform. Samantha was really ready for a break, too, but Robbie wasn't even breathing hard. Didn't the guy ever slow down?

"Listen, Robbie," Samantha said. "I saw a soda machine out in the hallway when we came in. I'm going to get one while you talk to the band, all right? I don't think I could take the usual dance punch."

"Sure, Sammy. Catch you later," Robbie said.

When Robbie reached the platform, Lacey, who had been standing to one side, walked up to him. "Hi," she said, "I'm Lacey Dupree. I saw you with Samantha just now. You must be one of the producers of 'Fast Takes.'"

"Right. Robbie Bodeen," Robbie said. "Are you with the band?"

Lacey shook her head. "I'm a friend of Tom Stratton, the leader. And I'm trying to help them with publicity."

"Shouldn't be too hard," Robbie said. "They've got a terrific sound."

"Oh, great, I'm glad you think so," Lacey said. "Come on, I'll introduce you to everybody." She and Robbie stepped up onto the platform. "Tom?" Lacey called. "This is Robbie Bodeen, the guy Samantha was telling us about."

Tom and Robbie shook hands, and then Lacey introduced the rest of the band—Joe Morelli on drums, Dean Wyckoff on keyboard, and Neil Lang, who played second guitar.

Lacey listened for a while as Robbie and the band discussed the possibility of Robbie putting together a tape for them. Robbie sounded enthusiastic about it.

When it was almost time for the band to start up again, Lacey realized the guys hadn't had anything to drink on their break. She told them she'd get them each a soda so they could keep talking with Robbie.

After hopping off the platform, Lacey started through the crowded gym toward the hallway. She stopped short, her heart sinking. Straight ahead, just inside the door, were Rick Stratton and his new girlfriend, Katie Fox. Lacey didn't know why she was surprised to see them—after all, Katie went to Southside. What she couldn't understand was why Rick would want to be anywhere Tom was playing. The two brothers hadn't spoken a word to each other since the horrible fight they'd had a few weeks earlier. Katie must have talked Rick into coming.

Lacey started to turn around, but it was too late. Katie and Rick had seen her.

"Hi, Lacey," Katie said. With amber eyes and long dark hair, she was so small and delicate that she made even Lacey feel clumsy. Lacey knew everyone thought Katie was sweet and friendly, but whenever the two of them had been alone, Katie's other personality had come out. She hated Lacey.

"Hi, Katie," Lacey said. She glanced at Rick. "Hello, Rick."

Rick barely nodded at Lacey before turning his full attention to Katie. "I think I'll get some air," he said. "Be back in a minute."

Katie watched him go before refocusing on Lacey. Her expression was no longer friendly, and her dark eyes were cold jet stones. "I don't suppose you were just leaving, were you?" she said.

Lacey shook her head. "Sorry."

"That's too bad," Katie said. "I suddenly need some fresh air, too." She whirled around and followed Rick out.

Lacey took a deep breath and let it out. Why was she the only one who knew what sweet Katie Fox was really like?

Taking another deep breath, Lacey stepped into the hallway and bought five cans of soda. Samantha Daley was there, and she volunteered to help Lacey carry the cans back to the band.

"Listen, we've got to start up again in a couple of minutes," Tom was saying to Robbie when Samantha and Lacey arrived.

"Sure, I understand," Robbie said. "We'll finish this later."

"So what happened?" Samantha asked Robbie. "Are you going to tape Mock Three?"

"Well, we've got some details to work out," Robbie said. "But it looks like we're going to put together a rock video and I'm going to direct it."

"That's great!" Lacey said. She handed a soda to Tom and gave him a quick kiss.

"Great is right," Robbie agreed. "The band will get the publicity, and I'll get a shot at directing." He turned to Samantha. "Thanks for setting this up, Sammy. I owe you one!"

And you'd better not forget it, Samantha added silently. Robbie Bodeen had better return the favor when it came time to pick the "Fast Takes" host.

Terry sighed as she poured soap powder into the dishwasher. Saturday night, she thought glumly. Everybody in the world was out on a date. Dancing at Commotion, going to the movies, eating pizza. Or just staying at home and watching a video, sitting close together on the couch in a darkened living room.

Oh, stop it, Terry told herself. She slammed the door to the dishwasher shut and pushed the Start button. Not everybody in River Heights was out on a date. There were plenty of girls—guys, too—who didn't have dates. She wasn't the only one. It just felt like it.

With the dishwasher humming away, Terry took a sponge and wiped the counters, then poured some dry food into the cat dish. Ashes, her gray cat, glided in through the door, rubbed against her leg, and settled down to eat. Terry watched him for a minute, thinking about what she could do for the rest of the night.

There were plenty of things. Read, watch TV, work on her room. She had always shared a bedroom with her sister, Vicki. Now Vicki was away at college and Terry was in the middle of redecorating the room just for herself. She thought of herself as an only child now—it was kind of fun. The past weekend she'd painted it white, and hung bright yellow curtains at the window. Her father had cut new shelves for her; she could paint those or hang pictures. Maybe she should take down the pictures of Vicki— especially the one of her sister, slender and beautiful, at last year's senior prom with her gorgeous date.

But Terry didn't feel like working on her room. "Boring," she said out loud. Ashes flicked his ears but didn't stop eating.

If only she hadn't gotten caught up in her big lie about Mickey Shaw, she could be out with her friends right then. Of course she'd be a fifth wheel, as usual. But when Karen and Ben were double-dating with Ellen and Kevin, as they were that night, they'd often ask her to come along. Not this weekend, though. Karen had teased her about her weekend plans. "I guess we won't be seeing *you* at all," she'd said. "You and Mickey probably won't resurface until Monday morning."

Terry had just smiled. Now here she was, stuck in the house. Well, she didn't want to be the odd person out, anyway. She'd find something to do, and by Monday, she'd have thought up plenty of juicy details about her fabulous weekend with Mickey.

"Teresa?" Mrs. D'Amato walked into the kitchen, buttoning up her black wool coat. "Oh, here you are. We're leaving now, honey." She checked in her coat pockets and pulled out a pair of gloves. "Your dad's warming up the car. He's probably griping to himself about going to this party." She laughed, her brown eyes crinkling at the corners. "I don't know why he hates open houses so much. I think they're fun. People coming and going, lots of goodies to eat."

"Daddy hates canapés and crowds," Terry said. "He'd rather fix himself a turkey sandwich and eat it alone."

Mrs. D'Amato sighed. "I know. But I promised the Bensons we'd come. Besides, if I don't drag your father out of the house once in a while, he'd sit here and turn to stone."

Mrs. D'Amato kissed Terry on the forehead. "What about you?" she asked. "Why don't you come? The Bensons said you're welcome."

Terry shook her head. There was nothing worse than being the only teenager in a room full of adults. Besides, they'd probably all wonder why she was there instead of being out with her friends. "Thanks, Mom, but I've got lots of things to do here," she said.

"You're sure?" Mrs. D'Amato raised her eyebrows.

Terry nodded firmly. She knew her mother worried that she didn't go out much, but she didn't want her mom feeling sorry for her. Terry could do that all by herself.

"Really, I'd rather stay here." Terry gave her mother a playful push toward the door. "You have fun. And don't let Daddy talk you into leaving twenty minutes after you get there."

Blowing Terry a kiss, Mrs. D'Amato hurried out of the kitchen, her scent perfuming the air. Terry heard the front door slam, and then the car pull away.

Finished with his meal, Ashes had planted himself by the back door. When he noticed Terry looking at him, he meowed. Terry opened the door and watched the cat slink off, melting into the shadows.

Wandering into the den, Terry saw the *Casablanca* tape sitting on the coffee table.

She'd rented it on Thursday, but she still hadn't watched it. At least it wasn't a new release, so the late charges wouldn't be too high. She picked it up, trying to decide whether she was in the mood for it.

Why not? *Casablanca* was a great romantic movie. She was paying for it, she might as well enjoy it. She slipped the tape into the VCR, then went back to the kitchen for a can of diet soda. Cold, Ashes was scratching at the door already, so she let him in. He walked with her back into the den, winding himself between her feet.

Terry pushed the Play button, then settled down on the couch. Ashes leapt up and joined her, curling up on the back of the couch, most of his weight against her shoulder.

Terry realized she'd made a mistake the minute the movie started. With the first notes of music, her eyes started to fill up. She'd go through three boxes of tissue before it was over. Terry pushed Stop on the remote control, then shut off the television and stared at the blank screen.

Mickey, she thought. If there was a Mickey, what would she be doing right then? Waiting for him to get here, she decided. He would be coming in about twenty minutes. They'd rented *Casablanca,* to watch together in her den. Her parents were at an open house, so they'd have plenty of privacy. After dinner, Terry would have washed her hair and then used some mousse on it. Not much, just enough to give it some style. She would have worn her tiger's eye earrings and the chocolate brown sweater with the gold threads running through it. Mickey really liked that one. He was bringing some of his homemade pizza. Terry smiled, thinking of how she'd tease him about it. She'd made some popcorn as a back-up.

Mickey would kiss her when he got here, and it would be at least fifteen minutes before they got around to watching the movie. Then they'd sit on the couch, close together, holding hands. Terry smiled again. They probably wouldn't see much of *Casablanca*.

In the darkened den Terry squinted down at her watch. Mickey would be there any minute. She strained her ears, listening for the sound of his Mustang. When she heard it, she got up and hurried down the hall to the front door. She wanted to be there, watching as he came up the front walk, his blue eyes lighting up when he saw her.

But when Terry opened the front door, a blast of cold wind hit her, bringing her back to reality like a slap in the face.

She couldn't believe it! For a few minutes, she'd actually tried living her own fantasy. She shut the door and walked slowly back to the den, where Ashes stared at her with wide topaz eyes.

"I almost lost it, Ashes," she said to him. "For a few seconds, I was completely crazy."

Okay, she thought, popping open her can of soda. It was time to come clean. Pretending was one thing, but when you actually started to believe what you were pretending, you were in major trouble.

On Monday she'd tell Karen and Ellen there was no Mickey Shaw. No blue eyes, no red Mustang, no hot romance. When they asked her why she'd lied, what would she say? That she'd thought they felt sorry for her? Terry shuddered, but she had to do it. She wanted a boyfriend, sure, but she'd never get one if she totally flipped out!

Too bad the big romance was over, she thought ruefully, scratching Ashes between the ears. She and Mickey had had a beautiful relationship, while it lasted.

9

On Monday morning Terry got off the bus and walked slowly toward the quad. The moment of truth was almost upon her, but she wasn't going to rush it. Maybe Karen and Ellen had already gone inside. That would give her until lunch to work on her confession. She'd spent most of Sunday trying to decide whether to tell them the truth, or to say that she and Mickey had broken up. She'd save her pride a little by saying they'd broken up, but then she'd have a lot more questions to answer. She'd have to put on a broken-hearted act, too, which would be another lie. One way or another, though, she was going to have to get it over with.

Once she reached the quad, Terry saw her friends immediately. They were talking and laughing, probably telling each other what fabulous weekends they'd had. Oh, well.

The truth, Terry decided. She'd tell them that she'd lied and was sorry. Straightening her shoulders, Terry forced herself to walk more quickly. If she slowed down now, she might chicken out.

Ellen saw her first and waved. Then Karen waved, too, beckoning Terry to hurry. Terry pasted a smile on her face and headed toward her doom.

"Guess what?" Karen said excitedly as soon as Terry was within earshot. "I had a great idea. You're going to love it."

"Listen," Terry began nervously. "I have to tell you—"

"Better let Karen tell you first," Ellen broke in. "She thinks nobody ever gave a party before."

"Well, *I* never have," Karen said.

Terry's mind was so focused on her confession, she could only stare at them blankly.

"For Ben," Karen explained. "His birthday's Thursday, so I'm having a party Friday night at my house. Do you think it's a good idea?"

"Sure," Terry agreed. "Sounds great. Listen—"

"Ellen and Kevin, Tim and Nikki, Calvin and Robin, Lacey and Tom, if Lacey's not working—" Karen rattled the names off.

"Plus Phyllis Bouchard and some other people."

"And you and Ben," Ellen reminded her.

"Right. And"—Karen pointed at Terry— "you and Mickey!"

Oh, no. Terry felt her face get hot.

Ellen gave Terry a gentle punch on the shoulder. "Come on," she teased. "You can't keep him under wraps forever. We're dying to meet him."

"And it won't be a big bash or anything," Karen said. "Just a few friends, so he won't feel lost. They're all really nice, you know that."

"Sure," Terry said, her mind racing. How was she going to turn this conversation around? "It's just that—"

"Don't tell me Mickey works on Friday night," Karen interrupted. "Because even if he does, it doesn't matter. He can come late." She paused, frowning a little. "Wait a minute —didn't you say he only works until nine on Fridays?"

Did she? Terry couldn't remember. She'd said so many things, it was impossible to keep track of all of them.

"That's right, I remember now," Karen said. "You told me you watched videos on Friday nights. So this will work out perfectly."

"Um—" Terry took a deep breath.

"There's just one thing." *Now,* she ordered herself. Tell them now.

But before she could get a single word out, Ben and Kevin arrived. "Hey, hey," Kevin said, draping an arm around Ellen's shoulders. "I bet I know what you guys are up to. You're planning some joke to play on Ben at his party." Kevin grinned. "So what's it going to be? A mud cake? One of those presents with about twenty boxes, all stuffed with newspaper? Check with me later, after Ben's gone. I'm a master at this."

"Forget it," Karen said, and slipped her arm through Ben's. "Ben made me promise we wouldn't do anything like that."

"Right," Ben said. "This is going to be a civilized party. Friends, food, music, talk. No practical jokes."

"You're no fun," Kevin complained goodnaturedly. He turned to Terry. "Hey, I hear we're finally going to get to meet the mystery man."

Terry nodded. Of course. Ellen and Karen would have told Ben and Kevin about Mickey.

"You guys are going to come, aren't you?" Ben asked Terry.

"Of course they are," Karen said. "It's all set."

"Right." Terry smiled weakly. "I can't wait."

"Wait a sec," Ellen said. "Terry, weren't you going to tell us something?"

Too late now, Terry thought. "Yeah, but I can't remember what it was." She shrugged.

When the bell rang, Terry lagged behind the others, pretending to search for something in her shoulder bag. She'd really done it now, she thought. Talk about party tricks! Making up stories about Mickey Shaw was one thing. Showing up at Karen's party with a guy who didn't exist was going to be the biggest trick of all!

Brittany was having a miserable Monday. Every time someone wished her good luck on the host job, she almost screamed. She couldn't possibly trust something so important to luck. She was used to taking charge and making things happen. Having to sit back and keep her fingers crossed was driving her crazy.

Walking down the hall between second and third period, Brittany kept her smile in place, but inside she was feeling more and more frantic. DeeDee was still out sick and might be all week. Of course, she'd see the tape of the final audition and she and Robbie would make a decision together. But if DeeDee wasn't around, it would be impossible for Brittany to influence her.

Why did DeeDee have to get sick now?

Brittany fumed to herself. And how bad could her flu be, anyway? If DeeDee would just drag herself to school, she'd probably forget how rotten she felt.

"Hey, Brit!" Robbie Bodeen's voice broke into Brittany's thoughts. "Glad I caught you," Robbie said. "The audition's all set. Thursday, okay? Right after school. Sammy first, then you. DeeDee and I'll go over the tape Thursday night. We'll post the results on Friday."

"Fine," Brittany said. "Listen, Robbie, you told me at the mall that this segment was going to be different." Brittany gave him what she hoped was a sweet and earnest look. "It would really help if I had *some* idea of what it's going to be. You don't have to tell me everything, naturally."

Robbie shook his head. "Sorry, Brit. I mean, if I told you anything, I'd be giving it all away. Then you'd be able to practice and have an edge over Sammy."

Brittany pretended to agree that it wouldn't be fair to Samantha. But Robbie had said "practice." What could that mean?

"Oh, well," Robbie said. "I *did* give Sammy a little hint, so I might as well give it to you, too." He repeated what he'd told Samantha, about taking the word *cut* literally.

The hint didn't mean much to Brittany,

but she was immediately suspicious. Why had Robbie told Samantha first? Was something going on between the two of them?

"Well, thanks, Robbie," she said. "It's nice to know you're being so fair minded. When exactly did you give this hint to Sammy?"

"Saturday night." Robbie cocked a finger at her and headed off again. "Catch you later, Brit."

Brittany felt as if the breath had been knocked out of her. Saturday night? That could mean only one thing. Samantha had somehow managed to get her hooks into Robbie Bodeen. From the expression on Robbie's face, they'd had a great time. Now he'd be on Samantha's side. What a sneaky rotten thing to do! She should have known Samantha would use every trick in the book to get the job.

Still fuming, Brittany sat through her English class, trying to decide what to do. DeeDee was out sick. Robbie was tilting toward Samantha. Who else could she work on?

By lunch Brittany still hadn't come up with any brilliant scheme of her own. When she saw Kim sitting alone, she joined her, glancing around warily. "Where's the snake?" she asked.

"If you mean Samantha, she's in the library, cramming for a test," Kim said.

"Good." Brittany sat down and unwrapped the plastic from her fruit salad. "Seeing her would ruin my appetite."

Kim groaned. "I wish you two would stop this. I'm stuck in the middle, remember?"

Brittany gave her a sour look. She didn't have much sympathy for Kim's predicament. "Do you know what she did?" she asked.

Kim sighed. "Samantha went after the lost job behind your back."

"Not just that," Brittany said. She swallowed a bite of pineapple and then told Kim about Samantha's date with Robbie. "How low can she get?" Brittany finished.

"Come on, Brittany," Kim said. "You're just mad because you didn't think of it first. Anyway, it wasn't really a date."

Brittany looked at her suspiciously. "You mean you knew about it?"

Kim clapped her hands over her mouth. "Oops," she said guiltily.

"You *did,*" Brittany said accusingly. "And you didn't tell me."

"I couldn't tell you," Kim said in exasperation. "I didn't know about it until afterward, and she made me promise not to tell."

"Well, you just broke your promise, so tell me everything now," Brittany demanded.

"Okay." Kim sighed. "Samantha took Robbie to a dance at Southside to hear Tom

Stratton's band. She knows Robbie's all hot
to do a rock video, and she wanted to make a
good impression by showing him Tom's
band. She admitted it. But it wasn't a date.
She says Robbie drives her up the wall.''

Brittany wasn't impressed. ''So what if it
wasn't a date? It was still fighting dirty.''
She leaned forward. ''She didn't happen to
find out what the audition's going to be, did
she?'' she asked tensely. ''If she knows and I
don't, I'm in big trouble.''

Kim shook her head. ''She said Robbie
clammed up when she tried to find out. I
don't think she was lying, either.''

Slightly relieved, Brittany ate some more
fruit. But the traitor was still one step ahead.
Brittany had to catch up, somehow. Drumming her fingers on the table, she scanned
the cafeteria. Suddenly she saw Dylan Tager
in the hall through the doorway. ''Dump my
tray for me, will you?'' she said to Kim. ''I
think I just got lucky.''

Hurrying past the crowded tables, Brittany sped out the door. There he was, just
about to turn the corner. ''Dylan!'' she
called, tearing down the hall after him.
''Dylan, wait!''

Dylan stopped and whirled around. When
he saw Brittany, his poster-perfect face broke
into a smile.

''Dylan,'' Brittany said breathlessly, coming to a stop about a foot from him. "I'm glad I saw you." She stepped closer and put a hand on his arm. "I just wanted to thank you for making the auditions so easy for me."

"Really?" Dylan raised his eyebrows. "You didn't seem to need any help at all."

"Oh, but I did," Brittany said. "I was scared to death, but you were just so relaxed, it was impossible to stay nervous." She tilted her head and gazed up at him.

Dylan smiled at her, his golden brown eyes warm. "If I helped, I'm glad," he said. "Let's hope I can help on Thursday, too. Of course," he added with a chuckle, "I might need some help with that one myself."

Bingo, Brittany thought. He knows what the audition segment's going to be. She knew not to push right then. It would be too obvious. She squeezed Dylan's arm, then stepped back. "Well, I guess I'd better be going," she said. "I'm glad I got the chance to thank you."

"Me, too."

Brittany was five steps away from him when she heard him say, "Brittany?"

Wiping the grin from her face, she turned around. "Yes?"

"I was wondering," Dylan said. "I know it's Monday night, but maybe we could grab an early dinner tonight."

Brittany arranged her face in a surprised,

pleased expression. "Why, thanks, Dylan. I'd love to." Tonight, she thought triumphantly. By the end of the evening, she'd know what the audition segment was going to be. Then she'd be able to practice for it, and Samantha wouldn't stand a chance. Brittany finally knew she had the host job all sewn up.

10

"So what kind of cake should I have?" Karen asked. "Chocolate with mocha icing? I think I can make that. Of course, when I cook it's usually a disaster. Maybe I should buy an ice-cream cake."

"Mmm," Terry said absently.

The two of them were in Terry's kitchen after school on Monday, discussing the plans for Ben's party. Or rather, Karen was discussing the plans. Terry was sitting in a state of near-panic, trying to come up with an excuse for not going. But the more she tried, the more her mind slowed down. She couldn't think of anything at all.

"Terry?" Karen leaned across the table. "Are you with me? I don't think you're really concentrating."

"What?" Terry blinked. "Oh, sorry. I was just thinking about something else."

"Mickey, I bet," Karen said with a grin.

Terry smiled weakly. "How'd you guess?"

"You can't fool me," Karen said. "I'd know that glassy-eyed, crazy-in-love look anywhere."

She had the crazy part right, Terry thought. She gave herself a mental shake and took a handful of pretzels. "Never mind. Ask me the question again."

"Homemade chocolate cake with mocha icing," Karen said. "Or an ice-cream cake from the Frostee Freeze?"

"What does Ben like?"

"Well, he likes ice-cream cake. But even though I'm a klutz in the kitchen, I'd like to make the cake myself," Karen said. "It'll be more special, I think."

"That's it, then," Terry said.

"I'll bake it Thursday night." Karen munched some pretzels as she wrote on a yellow legal pad. "Now decorations. We'll be in the family room, and it's got that high ceiling. I can hang crepe paper streamers from it, and balloons. What do you think?"

"Great!" Terry forced herself to sound enthusiastic, but the only thing she really wanted was to crawl into bed for a week and escape from everything. She couldn't tell the truth now, not with Karen so excited about the party. And anything else would be another lie.

"I know," Karen said. "Let's go to the mall tomorrow or Wednesday and hit the Party Stop. They have great decorations and stuff." She chewed on her pencil. "We could go to Glad Rags, too. I really need a new outfit. What about you?"

"Me?"

"Do you want to buy something new to wear?" Karen asked. "Not that you have to, but it could be fun."

"Oh, sure." Of course. Terry definitely needed to look fabulous for a phantom boyfriend. "I'm kind of broke right now, though."

"Me, too, I guess," Karen said with a sigh. "I'm hoping my mother will take pity on me and lend me some money."

At that moment Mrs. D'Amato came into the kitchen, her arms full of sacks of groceries. "Hi, girls," she said cheerfully, hefting the sacks up onto the counter. "Karen, it's nice to see you. How's your boyfriend? Ben, isn't it?" She pulled out milk and margarine and eggs. "Terry tells me he's really something."

"He is," Karen said. "As a matter of fact, I'm throwing a birthday party for him Friday night. Terry and I were just talking about it." She grinned and winked at Terry. "We're both broke right now, as usual," she said to Mrs. D'Amato. "We're trying to figure out what to wear to the party."

"Uh-oh," Terry's mother said. "I think I'm about to be hit up for a loan."

Terry started to protest, but Karen waved at her to shush. "Well, after all, Terry *is* bringing Mickey, and she wants to look extra fabulous."

Terry froze. Her parents knew absolutely nothing about "Mickey." How could they? But of course, Karen didn't know that. Terry held her breath, waiting for her mother to say "Mickey who?"

Mrs. D'Amato was putting things into the refrigerator, her back to the table where the girls were sitting. "Mickey?" she said distractedly, moving some containers around. "Well, I guess I could be persuaded to foot the bill for a new outfit."

Karen gave the thumbs-up to Terry, who managed a thin smile. Her mother must have misunderstood, that was it. How on earth was she going to figure a way out of this disaster?

At six-thirty that evening, Brittany and Dylan slid into a rear booth at Leon's. Even on a Monday the place was pretty crowded. Brittany knew that news of her date with Dylan would get back to Samantha, but she didn't care. Samantha was the one who'd started this war by trying to get Robbie on her side.

"Brittany, you look"—Dylan broke off, seeming to search for the right word—"really nice," he finished.

Nice was not exactly the word Brittany would have chosen. After all, she'd spent almost an hour rejecting outfits before settling on black leggings, an oversize black-and-gold sweater, and long golden earrings that brushed against her cheeks. Maybe Dylan was just too overwhelmed to think of a better word than *nice*. "Thank you," she said softly. She locked eyes with him for a few seconds, smiling seductively. "I'm starving," she murmured. "How about you?"

"Uh, sure." Dylan swallowed. "It's hard to think about food when you're sitting across the table from me."

Brittany gave a tinkly laugh. "Well, you're going to have to try," she said. "Here comes the waiter."

After ordering a cheese pizza and soda—diet for Brittany—the two of them talked a bit about school and classes and family. Dylan had an older brother in college. "Don took all kinds of advanced placement classes in high school," Dylan said. "Now he's going for his Ph.D. in microbiology. He has the brains in our family, I guess."

Brittany remembered DeeDee saying

something about Dylan not being very bright. If he was really clever, he'd have seen right through Brittany by now. As long as he wasn't a total idiot, Brittany didn't care. "Well, you must have gotten all the looks," she said admiringly.

"No, Don's good-looking, too." Dylan stopped, suddenly catching on that she was flattering him. He patted the empty space next to him. "Why don't you sit over here?" he suggested.

Brittany was up and on the other side of the table in a flash. "You're right," she said, scooting close. "This is much better."

The pizza came then, and after they'd each finished a slice, Brittany decided it was time to make her move. She leaned even closer. "Tell me," she said, "are you interested in a career in broadcasting, or are you doing 'Fast Takes' just for the fun of it?"

Dylan shrugged. "I never really thought about it one way or the other." He slid his arm along the back of the booth, his fingers touching Brittany's shoulder. "What about you?"

"I'm definitely interested," Brittany told him. "That's why I want the job on 'Fast Takes.'"

Dylan chuckled. "Well, you won't learn much about journalism from Thursday's audition, that's for sure."

"Oh?" Brittany's heart started pounding,

but she kept her voice calm and gazed at him steadily. "Why is that?"

Dylan shook his head. "A cooking demonstration isn't exactly my idea of a big story," he said, tightening his fingers on Brittany's shoulder. "I mean, Mrs. Edison helping us make stir-fried chicken and broccoli? Get real."

Brittany reached for her soda and took a big gulp. A cooking demonstration! And she was practically flunking home ec! DeeDee and Robbie couldn't have come up with anything worse. The flu must have really gotten to DeeDee's brain! And Robbie—well, she'd thought he'd at least want to do something exciting. Maybe the whole thing was Mr. Weston's idea.

"Hey, listen, I just remembered. I was supposed to keep the audition segment a secret," Dylan said, breaking into Brittany's thoughts. He rubbed his hand along her arm. "You won't tell, will you?"

"No, of course not," Brittany said automatically. She was busy thinking about how to handle a cooking show. Okay, don't panic, she told herself. Her cooking skills were limited, to say the least. But her mother stir-fried food a lot. She could teach Brittany everything she needed to know. This was Monday. If Brittany practiced for the next two nights, by Thursday she'd be an expert in stir-fried chicken and broccoli.

As for Samantha, Brittany knew for a fact that her ex-friend couldn't cook to save her life—or to get a TV host job, either, she added to herself with a triumphant smile.

Up in her room after dinner, Terry flopped down on her bed, letting her arms hang over the sides. *Think,* she told herself.

Unfortunately, Terry couldn't come up with a single way to dig herself out of this hole. It was only Monday, though. Maybe something would magically occur to her by Friday. Maybe she could suddenly come down with that awful flu that was going around.

There was a soft tap at the door. "Terry?" Mrs. D'Amato called. "I've got your clothes from the laundry room. You forgot to bring them up."

"Oh, thanks, come on in." Terry rolled over into a sitting position as her mother entered the room, her arms full of neatly folded clothes. Terry got up and took them from her. "Thanks," she said again.

"Listen," her mother said, as Terry started putting the clothes away in her dresser. "I didn't say anything when Karen was here, because I had the feeling you wanted to tell us yourself. But you didn't mention it at dinner, and I can't keep quiet any longer."

Terry turned around. Her mother had a big smile on her face.

"Mickey?" Mrs. D'Amato said. "Is that his name?"

Her heart sinking, Terry nodded.

"Well?" her mother asked, still smiling. "Tell me about him."

Terry cleared her throat. "There's not much to tell," she said slowly. "I don't know him very well yet. I mean, we've never gone out, actually. That's why I haven't said anything to you and Dad." Terry felt awful, lying to her mother. But her mother looked so pleased about Mickey, Terry couldn't bring herself to tell her the truth.

"So Friday is your first real date?"

"It's not even a date, really," Terry said. "He's just going to be at Karen's party. He works, so he'll be getting there later than I will."

"Oh, I see," Mrs. D'Amato said. "Well, I hope you have a great time." She slipped a hand into her skirt pocket and brought out two twenty-dollar bills. "For a new outfit," she said, pressing the money into Terry's hand. "Buy yourself something that'll make you feel terrific."

"Oh, Mom," Terry whispered.

"I know you said you're not really dating this boy, but maybe you will. I'm so happy for you, honey." Mrs. D'Amato smoothed

Terry's dark hair back, kissed her on the forehead, and left the room.

Terry clutched the money and swallowed hard, feeling incredibly guilty. For a guy who didn't even exist, Mickey Shaw sure did stir up a lot of excitement.

11

At lunch on Tuesday Brittany scanned the cafeteria and spotted Kim sitting with Jeremy. Samantha wasn't with them, so Brittany took her salad over to join them.

"You're looking a lot happier," Kim remarked, when Brittany sat down. "The last time I saw you, you were so mad I thought you'd explode."

"Things have changed since then," Brittany said, sticking a straw into her carton of juice. She tried not to sound smug, but it wasn't easy.

"Oh?" Kim raised her eyebrows and glanced at Jeremy. He knew all about Brittany's feud with Samantha, of course.

"What's going on, Brittany?" Jeremy asked. "What did you do, arrange to have

Samantha kidnapped so she'd miss Thursday's audition?"

"Very funny," Brittany said dryly. "That's not a bad idea, Jeremy, but, no, I haven't done anything to Samantha." Except beat her out of the host job, she added to herself. "I've just decided I can't go around being furious all the time. I'll just give the audition my best shot, and whatever happens, happens."

"You mean you've actually decided to forgive Samantha?" Kim asked, sounding skeptical.

Before Brittany could answer, Jeremy said, "Well, it's a good thing you've had a change of heart, Brittany. Here's your chance to prove it." He tilted his head toward the cafeteria line. Samantha was staring straight at the three of them.

Brittany immediately pushed back her chair and stood up. "I haven't had a change of heart at all," she said, picking up her tray. "I've just decided not to waste my energy thinking about what a rotten, low-down sneak Samantha Daley is."

Then, without another word, Brittany picked up her salad and moved to another table.

That evening Brittany cornered her mother in the kitchen and announced that she wanted to learn to cook.

Mrs. Tate was more than surprised. "Do you really mean it, dear?" she asked. "You've never shown an interest in cooking before."

"I know, but I guess it's time I did," Brittany said. "After all, when you work late, I should be able to help out more. And one of these days I'll be on my own. I can't live on cheeseburgers and pizza. I'll get fat."

Her mother laughed. "Well, okay, then. I'd be delighted to show you a few tricks. Let's see, what shall we make?"

"Stir-fried chicken and broccoli," Brittany said promptly. Her mother looked surprised again. "It's one of my favorites," Brittany added.

"Fine with me, if we have everything." Mrs. Tate checked the refrigerator and cabinets, mumbling to herself. "Chicken cutlets, broccoli, no scallions, but we can use a regular onion. Garlic, soy sauce, cornstarch." Soon the counter was piled with ingredients.

Brittany pointed to a twisted, knobby thing that looked like a small piece of pale, dead wood. "What's that?"

"Fresh ginger root," her mother said. "It makes the dish really tasty, much better than powdered ginger. You know," she went on, "stir-fried food is really good for you. You don't use much oil, and everything's cooked really fast, so all the vitamins remain."

Brittany nodded, taking mental notes. Mrs. Edison always made a big deal about nutrition. Brittany would be sure to mention it on Thursday.

"The key to stir-frying," her mother told her, taking out the cutting board, "is to get all the chopping and slicing done before you begin cooking. If you don't, you'll run into trouble." She looked at Brittany. "Okay, are you ready?"

"Sure," Brittany said, pushing up her sleeves. "Let's make dinner."

On Wednesday Karen spotted Terry in the hallway after third period and hurried over to her. "Don't forget," she said, "we're going shopping right after school. My mom lent me some money. What about you? Were you able to borrow some?"

"Yes," Terry said slowly. "But I'm not sure I should go."

"Why not?" Karen asked in surprise.

Terry didn't want to go shopping, that was why. She didn't want to spend her parents' money on an outfit for some guy who didn't exist. But she couldn't say that, not right there, not in the hallway. "Well, it's Mickey," Terry finally said. "He told me not to bother getting anything new. He likes the clothes I've got."

"Well, that's great," Karen said. "Except I'd really like you to come, anyway. You can help me pick out the paper plates and decorations and stuff."

"Oh, sure." Terry couldn't think of a reason not to do that.

"Good," Karen said. "Meet me in the student parking lot—I've got my mom's car." The bell rang and she started to turn away. "You know," she added over her shoulder, "it's really nice that Mickey likes the clothes you already have. He sounds like a great guy. I can't wait to meet him."

Terry headed toward her next class. Time was running out now. If she didn't tell the truth soon, she'd wind up at the party alone.

Maybe that's what she should do, she thought suddenly. Go to Karen's and pretend to wait for Mickey. Then, when he didn't show up, she could just leave. The next day she'd tell Karen and Ellen that they'd had a fight and broken up.

That was it, Terry decided. She'd go along with everything until Friday night. And by the end of the party, her romance with Mickey Shaw would finally be over.

By Thursday Brittany knew everything there was to know about stir-fried chicken and broccoli. She knew the trick of sticking the chicken into the freezer for a while, because it was easier to cut into thin slices afterward. She knew to peel the broccoli stems so they wouldn't be tough. She'd mastered the angle cut, and she could mince garlic with the best of them. Of course, she had a minor burn on her finger from spattering oil, and her eyes stung from onion fumes, but what were a few sacrifices on the road to success?

As she sailed into school Thursday morning, Brittany felt calm and serene. She was just a few hours away from being selected the host of "Fast Takes."

"She's up to something, I know it," Samantha said to Kim as Brittany passed them on her way to her first period class. Brittany had stared straight through Samantha, as if Samantha were invisible.

"She *does* look awfully confident," Kim agreed. "But you know Brittany—even if she were falling to pieces inside, she wouldn't let it show. Besides, what could she possibly be up to?"

Samantha chewed a fingernail as they walked down the hall together. "I don't know. Something."

"I think you're just nervous," Kim remarked.

"Of course I am," Samantha said. "I'm terrified! It's me against Brittany. Wouldn't you be scared?"

"Probably," Kim admitted. "But I don't

know if I'd be more scared of losing or winning."

Samantha's brown eyes widened. "I never thought of that," she said. "If I lose, I'll be totally disappointed. But if I win, Brittany will never forgive me. I don't know which will be worse!" she wailed.

"You could always drop out," Kim said.

Samantha stopped chewing her nail and stood up straighter. "No way!" she said fiercely. "I want this part, and I have as much of a right to try out for it as Brittany does." She became suspicious. "Did Brittany tell you to say that?"

"Say what?" Kim asked, frowning.

"That I could drop out."

Kim's nose twitched with indignation. "Absolutely not. I told you, I'm not taking sides in this. It was just an idea."

"Well, I'm not going to do it."

"Okay, okay, I get the point. If I don't see you at lunch, good luck," she said.

"Thanks." Samantha started to walk away, then turned back. "I suppose you're going to wish Brittany luck, too."

Kim nodded. "Sorry."

"I thought so," Samantha said. "Well, thanks anyway."

It didn't really matter that Kim was trying to stay friends with both her and Brittany, Samantha thought as she continued down the hall. If Kim could vote on the host, that would be different. But Kim's opinion didn't count. The only people who counted were Robbie and DeeDee. And Samantha, of course. In the end, it was really up to her.

As soon as the final bell rang, Samantha hurried to the closest bathroom, where she brushed her hair and put on some lip gloss. Then she stepped back and looked at herself in the mirror. Good. The weather was dry, and her hair hadn't frizzed at all. She had on a short corduroy skirt and her favorite sweater, a soft green. It wasn't her newest one, but it was the most comfortable. She didn't want to suddenly get stabbed by a label in the middle of the audition. Besides, the color was great on her.

Breathing deeply to steady her nerves, Samantha left the bathroom and headed for the AV room. As soon as she walked in, Robbie took her arm and steered her outside again.

"What's going on?" she asked nervously.

"We're setting up in a different place," he said, practically dragging her down the hall with him.

"Come on, tell me what's up," Samantha said.

Robbie laughed. "You'll see."

Samantha nervously hurried along beside him. What were they going to do? Shoot the audition outside or something? Maybe in the gym? If only she knew, she wouldn't be quite so worried.

Finally Robbie came to a stop. "Here we are," he said, pointing to an open doorway.

Samantha frowned. "This is the home ec room," she said.

"You got it."

Samantha stared at him. "This is a joke, right?"

"No joke, Sammy," Robbie said, ushering her inside. "For the final audition, we put together a little cooking show. Got an apron?"

If Samantha had one, she might have strangled him with it. At least now she knew what his hint about "cut" meant. But of all the things they could have done, this was the worst. She couldn't cook! She didn't know a frying pan from a saucepan, let alone that weird thing sitting on one of the stoves that looked like a flying saucer.

Samantha glanced around. Dylan and Mrs. Edison, the home ec teacher, were conferring about something. Alan, wearing a big pair of earphones that made him look like an alien, was fiddling with the tape deck. Cables snaked across the floor, and there were bright lights flooding one of the cooking alcoves. Under Mr. Weston's direction, three or four kids were scurrying around, taping down cables and helping check sound levels.

One girl held a microphone on a long pole over the kitchen area. This wasn't a joke. This was for real. Samantha knew she was doomed.

"Okay, Sammy, here's the deal," Robbie said. "Mrs. Edison's gonna make some chicken and broccoli in that wok, and you and Dylan will help out. How does that sound?"

Like torture, Samantha thought, drifting like a sleepwalker toward the cooking alcove. A wok, huh?

Suddenly Robbie got very busy, checking with Alan, directing the crew, consulting with Mrs. Edison and Mr. Weston. Samantha stood by in agony, wishing she could just fall through the floor and conveniently disappear.

In a few minutes everything was set. Robbie stepped behind the camera, and Samantha, Dylan, and Mrs. Edison took their places in the cooking alcove. "Okay, Mrs. E., you know what to do," Robbie said. "Quiet, please, everybody. Quiet on the set."

The room grew as hushed as a tomb. Robbie called, "Action." Mrs. Edison cleared her throat. "Hello," she said, a little too loudly. "Today, I'm going to make stir-fried chicken and broccoli, and I'm happy to say I have two kitchen helpers with me."

"Looks like a complicated dish," Dylan said, eyeing all the things on the countertop.

"Not at all," Mrs. Edison told him. "It's really very simple. Once you have the ingredients cut up, the cooking only takes about eight minutes."

"Fast food," Dylan said with a smile. "I'm impressed, aren't you, Samantha?"

Samantha almost jumped. For a few seconds, she'd actually forgotten they were being taped. Do it, she told herself. Just get the disaster over with.

"I sure am impressed," she said to Dylan. Her voice didn't shake, but her nervousness made her accent stronger than ever. "Why, my grandmother spends hours in the kitchen making chicken. Of course, she makes other things, too—cornbread and blackeyed peas, collard greens and sweet potato pie. It takes longer than eight minutes, but it's worth the wait." Actually, Samantha's grandmother did most of her cooking in the microwave, and Samantha had never eaten a collard green in her life.

"Well, I'm sure it's delicious," Mrs. Edison said. "But when you lead a busy life, this kind of cooking can save you lots of time. Let's get to it, shall we?"

"I'm ready," Dylan said, pushing up the sleeves of his dark blue turtleneck. "Just tell us what to do, Mrs. Edison."

There were three cutting boards on the counter. Mrs. Edison placed a bunch of scallions on one, a clove of garlic on another, and a raw chicken cutlet on the third. "To save time, I've already prepared the broccoli," she said, pointing to a bowl. "Now, while I slice the chicken, I want you, Dylan, to cut up the scallions. Samantha, the garlic's already peeled. All you have to do is mince it."

Sure, Samantha thought, staring at the pale little clove. She watched Mrs. Edison smoothly cut the chicken into thin strips. Then she looked at Dylan, who was slicing scallions as if he'd been doing it all his life. Finally Samantha picked up her knife and stabbed at the garlic clove, which went flying off the cutting board and hit Dylan square in the forehead.

The crew stayed quiet, but Samantha saw most of them grinning and trying not to laugh out loud. Well, she'd just go along with it. They already thought she was ridiculous, so she might as well give them something more to laugh at. She could feel humiliated later.

"Whoops!" Samantha said, laughing breezily. She made her accent even stronger. "Good thing it wasn't your eye, Dylan."

Dylan smiled and rubbed his forehead. "I can see you don't know your way around a kitchen, Samantha."

"Oh, you guessed my secret. Now everybody knows." The crew was stifling their laughter again, so Samantha tilted her head toward the camera and grinned.

"It's too bad your grandmother didn't teach you a few things," Dylan added teasingly.

"She tried, Dylan, but the day I ruined the sweet potato pie was the day she banned me from her kitchen forever."

Dylan stopped slicing scallions. "How'd you ruin it?" he asked.

"I forgot to peel the potatoes," Samantha shot back. Keep on joking, she told herself. You can crawl into a hole when it's all over.

By now, Mrs. Edison had not only finished with the chicken, but she'd peeled another clove of garlic and chopped it up into tiny bits. "Well," she said brightly, "Samantha, why don't you get the cooking sauce ready?" She handed Samantha a bottle of soy sauce, a glass measuring cup of water, a box of cornstarch, and a tin of powdered ginger. "I've written the measurements down here," she said, pointing to an index card.

"Think you can manage it?" Dylan asked, raising an eyebrow.

"You worry about *your* job," Samantha told him. She glanced at his cutting board, where the scallions were already finished. "I swear, Dylan, you chopped those things up like a professional chef. I'm impressed, I really am."

Samantha turned to pick up the soy sauce and accidentally knocked over the box of cornstarch. The white, floury starch whooshed up in a puff. Samantha started coughing and desperately waving her hands around, knocking over the soy sauce and water as well. Dylan patted her on the back while Mrs. Edison poured her a glass of water.

At last, Samantha stopped coughing and drank some water. The front of her green sweater was dusted with cornstarch, and soy sauce and water had dribbled down her skirt. She pushed her hair back and looked around. Dylan's place at the counter was immaculate, a little pile of scallions centered neatly on his cutting board. Samantha's place looked like a disaster area. The crew, and even Robbie, were holding their mouths shut to keep from hooting with laughter.

Looking directly at the camera, Samantha shrugged and said, "How about take-out instead?"

12

About ten minutes before her audition, Brittany, accompanied by Kim, leaned against the bank of lockers across from the home ec room. Pulling a small mirror out of her shoulder bag, she quickly touched up her lipstick and smoothed back a stray tendril of hair. She'd worn it in an intricate braid so no loose strand would fall into the food.

"This is really weird," Kim remarked, pointing to the closed door across the hall. "Home ec? Is it a cooking show or what?"

Brittany shrugged innocently. "Robbie sent one of the crew to tell me to come here, that's all I know," she said.

Kim chuckled. "What was your last grade in home ec, anyway?"

"B minus," Brittany lied. Actually, it had been a C plus, but close enough.

"And you're not worried?"

"That was last semester's grade," Brittany said, trying not to look smug. "I've improved since then."

Kim was about to reply when the door to the home ec room opened and Samantha emerged.

"Oh, no," Kim muttered, seeing Samantha's woebegone face.

Samantha's lower lip quivered as she dusted white powdery stuff off the front of her sweater and took off down the hall.

"I guess I'll see what happened," Kim said. "Good luck, Brittany."

"Thanks." Brittany waved at Kim and walked confidently into the home ec room. She didn't need luck. Thanks to two days of intense study in the fine art of chicken and broccoli, Brittany had skill on her side.

As she approached the cooking alcove, Brittany stopped and surveyed the scene. Two kids were sopping up spilled sauce on the counter, and a third was mopping the floor. The wok on the stove was smoking, and little pieces of scallion littered the area. Mrs. Edison was shaking her head in dismay, and Alan was worriedly checking the boom microphone that had been held far above the cooking alcove. "Grease," he muttered to no one in particular. "How'd she manage to splash the oil that far up?"

Everyone was chattering about Samantha.

Brittany bit back a smile of satisfaction. Samantha had obviously bombed.

As soon as he saw Brittany, Dylan came out from behind the counter. "Hi," he said, touching her shoulder. "Before we get started, I just wanted to tell you I really enjoyed our dinner the other night. How about getting together again soon?"

"I'd like that," Brittany said softly. "I can't wait." She wanted to ask him about Samantha's audition, to get the juicy, disastrous details, but she was afraid she'd start laughing hysterically and ruin her own audition. "Just give me a minute to prepare myself mentally," she said, leaning against him for a second. "I'm a little nervous."

"You'll be great," he told her. "And don't worry. I'll be right here with you."

All that flirting sure paid off, Brittany thought, watching him walk away. So what if he wasn't an Einstein?

In a few more minutes the kitchen was cleaned up and everyone was back at an appointed station. Robbie took Brittany's arm and steered her to the alcove, explaining what the audition was to be. Brittany listened intently, pretending the whole thing was a complete surprise.

"Okay. Places, please," Robbie called, going back to the camera. "Quiet on the set!"

"Wait a minute," Brittany said. "There's something stuck on my shoe." She bent down and peeled a small, pale, flattened object from the sole of her shoe. Holding it up to the bright light, she inspected it closely. "A garlic clove," she announced, wrinkling her nose. "I guess we won't need a garlic press."

There was laughter from the crew, and then Robbie called for quiet again. In a few more seconds Mrs. Edison had started her introduction. Brittany stood by quietly, alert and interested. When Dylan made his comment about fast food, Brittany knew exactly what to say.

"Stir-frying is definitely fast, Dylan," she agreed. "Not only that, but it's a hundred times more nutritious than a burger and fries." Then she went on to describe how the vitamins and flavors stayed in because of the quick cooking time, and how so little oil was used that the fat and cholesterol content were practically nil. "Isn't that right, Mrs. Edison?" she asked the home ec teacher.

Mrs. Edison was staring at Brittany, her mouth open slightly. "Well, it certainly is, Brittany," she said. "That's exactly what I was going to point out."

Dylan put his hand on Brittany's shoulder and gave it a squeeze. Brittany put her hand over his for just a second, then turned her attention back to Mrs. Edison.

The home ec teacher handed out the ingredients, explaining what she wanted Brittany and Dylan to do. Brittany got the garlic clove and minced it to bits in a flash. "That was fun," she declared brightly. "What else can I do?"

Surprised, Mrs. Edison gave her the ingredients for the cooking sauce. "Powdered ginger?" Brittany asked.

Mrs. Edison smiled apologetically. "I really recommend fresh ginger, but I brought all these ingredients from home and I didn't have any on hand."

"Fresh *is* better, I guess," Brittany said, speaking to the camera. "But powdered will do in a pinch!"

After that, things continued like clockwork. Brittany made insightful comments, asked questions, and moved gracefully around the kitchen alcove as if she'd been born in it. She was so competent that Dylan couldn't find much to say. He stood by admiringly, watching her with glazed eyes. The chemistry between the two of them was sizzling like the oil in the wok. Brittany smiled to herself. Samantha had never had a chance.

Finally Mrs. Edison spooned the food from the wok onto a platter. She tilted the platter slightly, giving the camera a view of the steaming chicken strips and crisp green broccoli. "There it is," she said, sounding pleased. "A beautiful and delicious dish, prepared in minutes."

"Cut!" Robbie called. "Okay, everybody, that's a wrap." He sped out from behind the camera and walked quickly to the cooking alcove. "Nice job, Brit. We'll let you know tomorrow."

Brittany went around the room, graciously thanking the crew. She knew she'd be working with them from now on, and it would pay to be on their good side. Then, with Dylan following in her wake, she swept from the room like a star.

Friday morning Samantha thought seriously about pretending to be sick. That day was going to be the most humiliating day of her life. Her audition had been an absolute horror, but now she realized that facing Brittany and admitting defeat would be even worse. She finally did drag herself out of bed and threw on some clothes. She might as well get it over with, she thought miserably. Why put off the inevitable?

Naturally when she arrived at school, everybody was talking about who the host would be. Samantha had to smile and say "thanks" whenever anyone she passed wished her luck.

When Samantha spotted Brittany talking to Kim on the quad, she panicked for a second. Maybe she should just go to the nurse's office. No, everybody had already seen her. If she left school now, they'd call her a coward as well as a failure.

Trying not to slink, Samantha made her way into the building. Then her heart sank even further. There, in the main hall way, was Robbie Bodeen, tacking a sheet of paper up on the announcement board. The paper would have Brittany's name listed as the host of "Fast Takes," Samantha knew.

"Samantha, you must be really excited," she heard a voice behind her say. Turning, she saw Cheryl Worth and Karla Todd. "I know I'd just be dying inside if I were you!" Cheryl added.

I *am* dying inside, Samantha wanted to say. "I know I didn't get it," she said.

"You'll never know until you look," Karla said. "Come on, let's go find out."

With Cheryl and Karla practically pushing her along, Samantha had no choice but to approach the bulletin board. Out of the corner of her eye, she spotted Kyle and Sasha. Oh, no, she thought. How much worse could things get?

"Go on, Samantha!" Cheryl urged.

Samantha stopped a few feet from the bulletin board and checked out Robbie's face. She couldn't get any clue at all from his expression. "I'm too nervous," she said. "Somebody else look at it for me."

"I'll do it," Karla said, marching up to the bulletin board.

Hurry up! Samantha wanted to scream. As soon as she heard the bad news, she'd get straight out of there.

But when Karla turned around, she had a big grin on her face. "It's *you!*" she shrieked. "You got the part, Samantha!"

Samantha blinked, not quite believing it. Then she stole another glance at Robbie, who was grinning and giving her a thumbs-up sign.

Suddenly the news sank in. She'd done it! Even after yesterday's horrible fiasco, they'd actually picked her to do "Fast Takes"!

Still stunned, Samantha stood frozen as the kids around her erupted into cheers and whistles and clapping. Cheryl Worth squealed and hugged her. Karla Todd slapped her on the back. Kyle didn't look at her, but that was all right. She knew he had to be impressed.

For a fleeting second, Samantha wondered how Brittany would take the news. But then she forgot about everything else and just listened as the kids continued to cheer around her.

After homeroom Kim caught up to Brittany as fast as she could. "Tough break," she said sympathetically.

"Oh, what do you care?" Brittany said. "You've been on Samantha's side from the beginning."

"I haven't been on anybody's side," Kim protested.

"That's even worse," Brittany snapped.

Kim sighed. "Maybe I'll just leave you alone for a while."

"Sure, go ahead and congratulate Samantha!" Brittany said, walking away in a huff.

She couldn't believe it! After all her hard work and sacrifices, after actually burning her finger and mincing garlic until she couldn't see straight, Brittany had lost. To *Samantha!*

If it weren't for Samantha Daley, Brittany's name would have been up on the bulletin board. Brittany would be receiving congratulations right now instead of pity. It was all Samantha's fault.

Fuming, Brittany strode around a corner and almost ran into Matt Schiller. "Brittany," he said. "I've been meaning to talk to you."

Brittany managed a small smile. "Me, too, Matt. Don't think I've forgotten about our date."

"Well, that's what I wanted to talk to you about," he said. "I was at Leon's Monday night."

"Monday?" Brittany swallowed. That was when she'd been snuggling up to Dylan, for all the good it had done her. "Well, I can imagine what you must have thought, but it wasn't like that, Matt."

"Well, I hope not," Matt said coolly. "Catch you later, Brittany."

Brittany's shoulders drooped. Had she blown her chances with Matt? She couldn't tell for sure. Of course, she had Dylan Tager interested in her, but he was probably going to be busy all the time with "Fast Takes." Thanks to Samantha, Brittany's career and love life were both less than zero.

"Brit! Hey, Brit!"

Gritting her teeth, Brittany turned around to face Robbie Bodeen. "Yes?" she said.

"Listen, I wanted to tell you how great you were yesterday."

"Oh?" Brittany raised her eyebrows. "Samantha must have been Oscar material, then."

Robbie shook his head. "It's not that she was better. Actually, she—" He broke off and laughed while Brittany tapped her foot impatiently. "Sorry," he said, wiping his eyes. "You had to be there."

Brittany was glad she hadn't been. "You were saying?" she asked.

"Yeah, well, DeeDee and I decided to go with Sammy because of the chemistry thing," he explained. "You and Dylan had it, all right, but it was the wrong kind." He whistled and wiggled his eyebrows. "Sexy stuff, but not what we need. See, Sammy and Dylan kind of joked around, traded insults, know what I mean? It was loose, funny, lots of kidding."

"I see," Brittany said. Robbie was just making things worse by explaining.

"Right. But listen, you were great. DeeDee and I were thinking we could use you in other ways," he said. "Maybe work you into a semiregular reporting spot. How does that grab you?"

Brittany stared at him. A *semiregular* spot? Did he really think she'd be satisfied with that? "My schedule's awfully full," she said with a shrug. "You'll have to check with me when you have it worked out and I'll see if I have the time."

"Great, will do." Robbie grinned and punched her softly on the arm. "Like I said, Brit, you were great. It was a tough break for you, but that's show biz." He cocked his finger at her and spun around, hurrying off down the hall.

Brittany walked on, thinking. Her schedule *was* full, she realized. After all, she still had her column for the *Record*. And DeeDee would start working with the next editor-in-chief pretty soon, which was a much more important job than being a host on "Fast Takes." It had been ridiculous to go after the host job, really. Compared to serious journalism, it was a piece of fluff. Brittany didn't know why she had even tried out for it.

Turning another corner, Brittany suddenly found herself staring down the hall at Samantha. Even though Brittany had now convinced herself she'd never even wanted the host spot, she still wasn't ready to forgive Samantha. No one stabbed Brittany Tate in the back and got away with it.

Seeing Brittany, Samantha stopped walking, her smile gone. Brittany could tell she was worried, trying to figure out what Brittany would do. Snub her? Shriek at her? Vow revenge?

Brittany glided smoothly toward Samantha, and when she was a few feet away, she smiled. "Congratulations," she said loud enough for anyone within a hundred feet to hear. "You'll do a great job."

Without waiting for Samantha to reply, Brittany swept off, shoulders back, head high.

Samantha looked after her, not fooled a bit. There was no question about it. Brittany was really on the warpath now.

 **13**

Sitting beside her father as he drove her to Karen's house on Friday night, Terry actually found herself wishing he'd go a little faster. She was hardly thrilled about the upcoming evening, but the sooner it was over, the sooner she could forget about it and put all the lies behind her.

She'd thought about her plan some more and decided it would work. She'd wait until about ten. Then, when Mickey didn't show, she'd tell Karen she'd been stood up. Then she'd go home. On Monday she'd say she'd decided not to see him anymore. From then on, Mickey Shaw would be history.

Her father glanced at her as he turned a corner. "What time do you think you'll be getting home, honey?"

"I'm not sure, Dad." Not late, she thought.

"Got your key?"

He wouldn't be satisfied until she checked, so Terry opened her bag and fished around for her keychain.

"Your mother talked me into going over to the Wileys' for bridge, you know," her father went on. "I don't know how late we'll be."

"Well, I can get in the house," Terry assured him, holding up her keys.

"Good." Mr. D'Amato drove silently for a moment. Then he cleared his throat.

Here it comes, Karen thought. She knew her dad must have had a reason to drive her to Karen's. Normally she'd just walk. He was building up to talk to her about something.

"Your mother told me about this new boyfriend of yours."

Terry shifted uncomfortably. "He's not really my boyfriend," she said. "I mean, we haven't even had a real date or anything. It's not as big a deal as Mom thinks."

Mr. D'Amato smiled. "Well, it can't be too small a deal, either. You're so dressed up and pretty. Not that you're not pretty all the time," he added quickly. "But you look extra nice tonight."

"Thanks, Dad." Terry glanced down at her new dress, which Karen had insisted she buy. It was a dark gold mini in a soft knit material, with long sleeves and buttons down he back. It had been on sale, and Terry was going to give her mother back the change, but Karen talked her into buying a pair of earrings, small golden rectangles that caught the light whenever she moved her head.

Terry knew she looked good. But when she found herself wishing she had somebody to look good for, she told herself to forget it. That's what had gotten her into this mess in the first place.

At last Terry's father pulled the car up in front of the Jacobses' house. Terry leaned over and kissed him on the cheek, feeling guilty for having lied to him and her mom. She said goodbye, got out of the car, and watched her father drive off. Then she walked up to the house and rang the doorbell.

Karen answered, looking great in a silky blouse and a short black velvet skirt. "Good, you're here," she said, pulling the door open wide. "Come on back. The family room looks great."

"How's the party going?" Terry asked, following her down the hall and waving to Karen's parents, who were watching TV in the living room.

"Fine, I guess," Karen said. She stopped and stared at Terry. "Emily's here."

"You're kidding," Terry said. "Why did you invite her?"

"I didn't," Karen said. "Ben suggested

that I invite Bill Hutchins, and Bill asked Emily." Karen sighed. "Ben *knew* Bill and Emily are going out now."

Terry shrugged out of her coat and draped it over her arm. "What are you thinking, Karen?" she asked. "That Ben *wanted* Emily to be here?"

"I don't know," Karen said, frowning. "Maybe."

"Come on, Karen," Terry said. "You know Ben loves you. He probably didn't stop to think about Emily at all. You're just imagining things. I bet you're tired. How late were you up baking that cake, anyway?"

"Until three," Karen admitted with a wry smile. "The icing was a disaster the first time and I had to make it over. You're probably right," she agreed with another sigh. "I'm just being paranoid. Come on, let's go have fun."

Everybody was in the family room, which was decorated with long blue streamers and balloons. Silver letters spelling out "Happy Birthday" were strung from the mantel above the fireplace, and a table covered with a blue paper cloth held platters of chicken wings, bowls of dip, chips, potato salad, and cut-up vegetables.

"Terry, hi!" Nikki Masters called when Terry came into the room. She was sitting on a big cushion in front of the fireplace. Her oyfriend, Tim Cooper, sat beside her, eating opcorn from a bowl. Phyllis Bouchard was a the other side of the room, gazing at Tim. mily and Bill were deep in conversation on e couch. "Get something to eat and come in us," Nikki said to Terry.

Terry waved to Nikki and got herself a can f soda from the table. She wasn't really ungry.

"Karen said your boyfriend's going to be oming later," Nikki said when Terry joined er and Tim.

"He's a Southside guy, right?" Tim asked. I know some kids from Southside. What's is name?"

"Mickey Shaw," Terry mumbled.

Tim thought a minute. "Nope. Doesn't ing a bell."

Nikki leaned her shining blond head gainst Tim's shoulder and smiled at Terry. "So when is Mickey getting here?"

"Oh, soon," Terry said. She smiled, too, nd moved away. She should have known Karen would tell everybody, but she didn't vant to discuss Mickey any more than she nad to. Especially since he was going to stand her up.

At the far end of the family room were Robin Fisher and her boyfriend, Calvin Roth, playing Ping-Pong and arguing about the score. Ellen and Kevin and Ben and Karen were watching them, with Kevin doing hi impression of a sports announcer. Lacey an Tom were snuggled on the loveseat, wit Neal Langley and his girlfriend standin behind them.

Phyllis was at the food table now, an Terry was tempted to join her. But then sh changed her mind. It would be to humiliating—the only two dateless girls stuffing themselves together.

Terry moved from group to group, chattin and laughing and checking her watch. Th minutes seemed to crawl by, but at last it wa ten o'clock. Karen had been giving her curi ous little looks for the last ten minutes, and Terry knew she was wondering why Mickey wasn't there yet. It was time to get this over with, she decided.

Catching Karen's eye, she waved her over and the two of them went into the kitchen "Listen," Terry said. "I don't think Mick ey's coming. He must have had to work late Video City's open until midnight."

Karen frowned. "Well, why didn't he call?"

Terry shrugged. "It doesn't matter. I think I'll go on home."

"Why?" Karen asked.

"Because it's embarrassing," Terry said. "You told everyone Mickey was coming— not that I blame you," she quickly added.

"But it'll look like I've been stood up
go back into the family room and face e
one."

Karen frowned again. "I still think he
should have called you," she said.

"He's kind of forgetful," Terry told her.
"Anyway, I think I'll just head home."

"No way," Karen said. "If Mickey's so
forgetful, then I think you should just go
remind him."

"What do you mean?" Terry asked. This
wasn't going the way she'd expected.

Karen was already getting the car keys
down from a hook near the telephone. "I
didn't buy enough soda, anyway," she said.
"We'll go over to Video City so you can tell
Mickey Shaw exactly what you think of him,
and then we'll get some more soda on the
way back."

"No, wait, I can't do that!" Terry cried.

"Yes, you can," Karen told her. "You have
to, Terry. Didn't you tell Mickey how all
your friends are dying to meet him and
everything?"

"Well, yes, but——"

"So he knew how important it was,
right?" Karen interrupted. "And then he
doesn't show up and doesn't even bother to
call." She sighed. "Look, I know I'm telling
you to do something that I probably wouldn't
have the guts to do myself."

...ry agreed.

...n't be alone," Karen went on. ... you, backing you up. And ...xt time *I* need to be brave about something, you'll back me up."

"Sure, but——"

"Come on," Karen said. "We both have to learn how to stand up for ourselves."

Taking Terry's arm in a firm grasp, Karen pulled her back into the family room, called to everybody that they were going to get more soda, and then dragged Terry to get her coat and out of the house to the car. Ten minutes later they were pulling into the brightly lit parking lot of Video City.

Karen shut off the car and started to get out.

"Wait," Terry said, thinking fast. "You're right, I should tell Mickey off. And I'm going to. But it's something I have to do by myself. Okay?"

"Okay," Karen said, nodding. "I guess you're right. Good luck."

Taking a deep breath, Terry got out of the car and went into the store. She had absolutely no idea what she was going to do when she caught sight of the guy who'd waited on her the week before. Brian, she remembered from his name tag. He was putting little "Out" tags on boxes of tapes. Terry looked him over quickly. His hair was brown. Not nearly so dark as Mickey's was supposed to be, but it would have to do. If Karen was watching through the window, maybe she'd think the light in the store made his hair look different.

Now for the hard part. Terry took another deep breath and walked over to Brian. "Excuse me," she said. "Could I talk to you for a minute?"

He smiled. His eyes were hazel, Terry noticed, but Karen couldn't see that far, and besides, his back was to the windows.

Brian was staring at her curiously. "I remember you," he said. "You rented one of those ancient movies last week. *Casablanca.*"

"Right," Terry said.

"You like old movies, huh?"

Terry remembered that he'd asked the same thing when she'd checked it out, as if he couldn't believe it. "I like a lot of them. Especially that one." She suddenly remembered she was supposed to be chewing him out, so she waved her hands around, hoping Karen would think she was angry. "It's great!" she said. "Haven't you ever seen it?"

Brian shook his head.

"Well, you should!" Terry pointed at him. People always pointed at each other in an argument. "You really ought to. You'd love it."

Brian stepped back. He was laughing, but

Karen couldn't see that, Terry told herself. She'd think he was backing away because Terry was so mad. Perfect.

"Okay, okay, I get the idea," Brian said, putting up his hands. "I'll take a look at *Casablanca.*"

Terry nodded. "Good."

Brian seemed to be totally confused.

Terry wished she could explain, but she decided she'd been there long enough. It was time to get out. "Well, that's all I wanted to say," she told him, turning away.

"Uh, wait."

Terry turned around. "Yes?"

"I just decided to watch it this weekend," Brian said. "Maybe we could talk about it sometime."

In a flash Terry realized he thought she'd been flirting with him. She felt herself blush in embarrassment. She'd never flirted with a guy in her whole life, and now she had a total stranger thinking she was after him.

Brian didn't seem to notice, though. "My name's Brian Sable," he said. "I go to Southside, but I've never seen you there. Do you go to River Heights High?"

Terry nodded, speechless. Even after the way she'd acted, he didn't think she was a total jerk.

Brian grinned at her. "Are you going to tell me your name, or do you want me to guess?"

Terry smiled, not really believing this was happening. "Teresa D'Amato," she said. "Terry."

"Terry," he repeated as if he liked the sound of it.

Terry still couldn't believe it. She hadn't even been trying to get this guy to notice her, but he had. Maybe it was because she *hadn't* been trying. Maybe that's what she should have done all the other times, when she'd felt so tongue-tied around boys. This was amazing.

"So what do you think?" Brian asked. "Can you come by tomorrow and stick around so we can talk for a while?"

"About *Casablanca?*" Terry asked.

"About anything," he said, blushing now, too. "To tell you the truth, I'd like to get to know you," he barely whispered.

Terry's heart started to beat faster. "Okay," she said, smiling at him. "I'd like that, too."

Brian had to help another customer then, so he said goodbye, after making her promise she'd come back. "I work one to six." Still in a daze, Terry was pulling open the door when she remembered Karen. What would she tell her now? She'd gotten so good at lying, it only took her a few seconds to think up a story about Mickey having lost Karen's address and forgetting her last name so he couldn't even call.

No, Terry told herself. No more lies, no more fantasies. She'd tell Karen the truth. Then, she thought with a little smile, she'd tell her about Brian Sable. He worked at Video City. He had brown hair, hazel eyes, and he'd never seen an old movie in his life. That's all she knew about him, so far.

But maybe after the next day she'd know more. And who knew? This might be the beginning of a beautiful relationship. Only this time, it would be real.

Back at Karen's house, the party was still going strong. Tom Stratton was more relaxed than he usually was in a crowd, and Lacey was glad. "You're really happy about that video, aren't you?" she asked him.

Tom nodded, squeezing her hand. "Robbie's going to be a major pain, but I have a feeling he knows what he's doing," he said.

"I think the video idea is great," Robin said excitedly. "Whose idea was it, anyway?"

"Lacey's, of course," Tom said.

"Well, it was really Samantha Daley's," Lacey said. "She was the one who brought Robbie to the Southside dance."

"Oh, is that where he heard you?" Robin asked. "You didn't tell me, Lacey."

"I guess I forgot." Lacey jumped up from the floor cushion. "I'm going to see if Karen's back yet with the soda," she said, hurrying off to the kitchen.

Robin followed her. "What's wrong?" she asked, coming into the kitchen behind Lacey. "You acted like I accused you of something."

"It's not that." Lacey sighed, tucking her reddish blond hair behind her ears. "I just didn't want to talk about Southside, that's all."

Robin's dark eyes narrowed. "You mean because of Katie?" she asked.

Lacey nodded. "She was there. With Rick. I ran into them."

Robin shifted impatiently. "Well, so what? Katie seems like a really nice person, and she's probably great for Rick. Why should that bother you?"

Lacey sighed. She couldn't believe it. Everybody felt sorry for Rick—even though he was the one who had broken up with Lacey. She wished they'd stop treating him like the injured party. Lacey was just plain sick of it. "It doesn't bother me that she's great for Rick," she said to Robin.

"Good." Robin grinned. "Actually, *I'm* the one who should be bothered by Katie," she said. "There's a swim meet coming up against Southside, and I'll bet she's going to be in it."

"Really?" Lacey took a deep breath. "Then I think you'd better look out, Robin. I have a feeling that sweet Katie Fox doesn't play fair at all."

First Katie Fox stole Lacey's boyfriend. Now will she take Robin away from her, too? Jeremy Pratt's sleazy friends Hal and Wayne have made a cruel bet—and Phyllis Bouchard may be the one who loses. Can Brittany Tate come scheming to her rescue? Find out in River Heights #16, *The Jealousy Trap.*